**"Because if I stay** while, and most of that time will be spent **doing what we should've been doing in the Bahamas. What we should've been doing long before the Bahamas."**

"I'm confused." She said the words while sharing a look that expressed just the opposite. Part of her hoped they would continue along this line of discussion. The other part of her anticipated him changing tactics on her once again.

"That's a shame." He pushed off the wall.

Ray pegged the edge to his soft voice as resignation, and she assumed their time together had reached its end. She stood, deciding to beat him to the door. Instead, she found her path blocked and then she was taken off her feet entirely.

"Where?" he queried against her cheek.

*Anywhere.* The initial response came to mind silently before she reconsidered. She'd stand a better chance of keeping him longer if he were in her bed.

*Desperate, Ray?* a voice jibed. So what if she was? She'd damn well earned the right to treat herself, and what better treat than over six foot five inches of well-defined dark onyx muscle with a stunning brain to match.

Dear Reader,

As you no doubt have heard, this will be my last title with the Harlequin Kimani Romance line. It has been a special treat getting to know wonderful readers like you, and I thank you for your support of me and my colleagues.

It's my joy and privilege to round out my Kimani publications with a special holiday story. *Seductive Moments* features Barker Grant and Rayelle Keats. The attraction has been simmering around this couple for far too long and the time has come for it to be explored. With the holiday season in full bloom, Barker and Rayelle give in to the passion between them and the intense situations surrounding them, and encounter a truly unexpected surprise in the midst of it all.

Thank you so very much for welcoming my stories into your life.

Peace, Love and Blessings Always,

*AlTonya Washington*

altonya@lovealtonya.com

# Seductive Moments

## AlTonya Washington

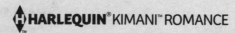

**H HARLEQUIN® KIMANI™ ROMANCE**

Recycling programs
for this product may
not exist in your area.

ISBN-13: 978-1-335-21690-8

Seductive Moments

**Printed in U.S.A.**

**AlTonya Washington** has been a romance novelist for fifteen years. She's been nominated for numerous awards and is the winner of two RT Reviewers' Choice Awards for her novels *Finding Love Again* and *His Texas Touch*. She won the Romance Slam Jam EMMA Award for her novel *Indulge Me Tonight*. AlTonya lives in North Carolina and works as a reference librarian. This author wears many hats, but being a mom is her favorite job.

### Books by AlTonya Washington

### Harlequin Kimani Romance

*Texas Love Song*
*His Texas Touch*
*Provocative Territory*
*Provocative Passion*
*Trust In Us*
*Indulge Me Tonight*
*Embrace My Heart*
*Treasure My Heart*
*Provocative Attraction*
*Silver Screen Romance*
*Seductive Memory*

Visit the Author Profile page
at Harlequin.com for more titles.

The final Kimani, but the stories do not end here.
Thanks to my readers who have followed
wherever my work has taken me.
I love and appreciate you guys so much!

# Chapter 1

*Philadelphia, PA*

"See? Perfect security and you're even asked for your autograph."

"It's for the missus, Ray."

"Sure it is, Ollie." Rayelle Keats sent a sidelong smile to the third-shift security guard of her apartment building.

"It's okay, Ollie. It's always a pleasure to meet the fans…and their husbands." Barker Grant looked up from signing his name to the pad he held.

Knowing he was being teased, Oliver Leaks favored the couple with a good-natured wave. "It's true, Mr. Grant." Oliver's ruddy weather-beaten face sharpened with distinct reverence. "She really does love your work—matter of fact, we both feel good know-

ing there's folks like you on the job gettin' the facts—
the *real* ones."

Barker nodded, reflecting a reverence similar to Oliver's expression. "It's nice to be counted on for that,
'specially when folks hardly see me on camera."

"Aw." Oliver gestured with another wave. "People
read those tiny credits the station puts at the bottom of
each story—your name's known, kid, trust me. Everybody knows who it is breaking WPXI's hardest cases.
Most of the viewing public are so in awe of the pretty
faces on screen, it's nice to know one of 'em's not afraid
to get out there and dig for the truth that makes the camera folk look even better than they do."

"Well, Ollie, I do believe I heard a compliment in
there." Barker returned the pad.

The cherub-faced seventy-year-old responded with a
bashful chuckle. "That's comin' from the missus, too."

"Well, thank her for that, okay?" Rayelle squeezed
the man's forearm.

"You two take care," Oliver called while the couple
headed for the elevator bank located behind the wide
semicircular lobby desk.

"You really didn't have to put yourself out like this."
Ray sighed as they approached one of the cars. "You
must be just as wiped as everyone else after that trip
back."

Barker's grin widened against his dark face. "Funny
how long the trip coming back from the Bahamas
seemed next to the one going there."

"Agreed." Ray's laughter echoed in the maple-paneled
corridor. "But that's my point," she said, sobering. "You
should head on home if you want to get a jump on some

sleep. I can handle a ride up to my place, and it's not like I need help with my bags."

Silently Barker agreed, eyeing the tall yet compact rolling case Rayelle pulled leisurely along behind her. His bottomless stare held the bag only a few seconds before easing back to its owner, where it had been pretty much fixed since they had deplaned.

Since deplaning? Barker allowed himself a mental eye roll. His eyes and practically every other part of him had been fixed on Rayelle Keats from the moment he'd seen her over a year ago across a crowded restaurant dining room. The leggy beauty with shoulder-length deep brown tresses that waved around a face the tone of light coffee had claimed a top spot in his mind ever since. He'd sent his things on ahead to his place, but there had been no real need for such fanfare. No need to join Ray for the ride to her home…

They had returned in the dark hours from the sun and dazzle of the tropics. Still, there'd been no real reason to worry she'd run into trouble without a male escort by her side. At any rate, he'd wanted to… He wanted…

Ridding his thoughts of the uncomfortable truth, Barker focused on her earlier comment. He noticed the expectant gleam in her eyes, which were the distinct color and shape of almonds.

"No one else went home alone. Why should you?" That was his simple argument.

Ray had no comeback for it. Besides, the words were true, weren't they? The Bahamas trip had been a couples' getaway, despite the fact that it had *technically* been two couples short at the time. Linus Brooks and

Paula Starker had been on the outs at the onset of the trip, but things had changed quite nicely.

Barker and Rayelle, while not on the outs, were still dancing around the fringes of the crush that had been idling in neutral for almost a year. The Bahamas had brought them closer in a platonic way that told Ray that Barker wasn't just a respected journalist; with the face and body of a sex symbol, he was a gentleman, as well.

That wasn't such an outlandish idea to grasp. Barker Grant was, after all, a local celebrity with a name that was highly regarded in national and international circles. The fact that they'd skirted around a strong and mutual attraction for several months was okay as far as Ray was concerned. Something told her that a romance with a woman who was a former-exotic-dancer-turned-gentleman's-club-manager-turned-dance-school-manager would be a tough sell.

It told her something else, too, or at the very least, made her wonder. Maybe Barker Grant just figured he was intuitive enough to know the word *gentleman* didn't quite make the list when one described the kind of men Rayelle Keats invited to her home. Ray wondered how stunned the intuitive reporter would've been to learn he was the first man to have made it past her front door in well over two years. *He only wanted to help you with your bags, Ray, jeez...*

Only...she didn't have any bags.

The car had arrived with a soft ding, and they made their way inside the cozy confines. Ray felt the case handle leave her grasp, and she saw that Barker had taken hold of it. She managed to smother the sound of her clearing throat, which often signaled her nervousness.

There was no need to confirm that his eyes were on her. She could all but feel the dark, deep-set orbs traveling along her skin. During their trip, she had discovered those orbs had hints of gray swirled amid the otherwise midnight hue. An intriguing asset, not that he needed any additional enhancements. His hair was the same shade as his gaze and waved soft and full over his head. His skin was a rich molasses tone that had Ray wondering if it felt as flawless as it appeared.

Again she cleared her throat and then searched her mind for appropriate elevator talk. All that came to her was the weather. She shivered then, huddling into the folds of her heavy shawl. "Sure is a temperature change from the tropics," she noted with a shimmer of laughter coating the words.

Barker's mouth tilted into a knowing smile. "This time of year has my family gearing up for their Christmas parties."

"Parties." Ray's eyes glinted with interest. "Sounds like they really get into the celebrating."

"Do they." Barker grinned his agreement. "My mom celebrates her birthday so...it gives everyone more of a reason."

"It sounds nice."

Barker didn't miss the undercurrent of longing in her words. He didn't pry, deciding to leave that particular task for later.

There was no time for prying anyway. The elevator was quickly making its ascent. "I really appreciate this, Barker," Ray said.

Barker realized then that she expected them to part ways once the doors opened. When they did, a woman waiting for the elevator gave a start at finding unexpected travelers there so early in the morning.

The warmth of familiarity crept into the woman's pale brown eyes when she saw Rayelle. That warmth turned into a sparkle of approval when she took note of the man at Ray's side.

"Well, well, love, this is a surprise. I was just asking security if they knew when you'd be getting back home. I was hoping to see you before the end of the holidays."

"Miss Amelia, remember I told you I'd be back by Christmas."

"No matter." Amelia Shepard lifted a slender shoulder. "I'm happy to have you home anyway." She pulled Ray into a quick, tight squeeze before stepping back to once again regard her neighbor's escort.

"I'm sure women try all kinds of lines on you, sweetness." Amelia tapped a gloved finger to her cheek. "But you do look very familiar. Have we met before?"

Ray shifted closer to the tiny woman. "Amelia Shepard, this is Barker Grant. He works for WPXI. Maybe that's how you know him."

"Mmm...no, I prefer WZHY—no offense, hon."

Barker and Rayelle lowered their heads to shield emerging smiles, but Amelia didn't appear to notice. She continued to tap at her cheek.

"WPXI...hmm..."

Ray eased an apologetic look toward Barker. "Miss Amelia—"

"Ah! I have it! You're one of the Delano Grants, aren't you?"

Ray's apologetic expression melded into one of extreme interest. She watched Barker's handsome face adopt a sheepish tint.

"Yes, ma'am," he said to Amelia and then looked to Rayelle. "Delano Grant was my grandfather," he told her.

"Well, I'll be!" Amelia looked tickled and clapped her hands once enthusiastically. "One of the Delano Grants in my very own hallway." She sent an encouraging look to Ray. "Treat him well, miss. He comes from a very fine family—very fine."

Though her curiosity was evident, Ray decided to bypass questioning her neighbor. They'd spend the better part of the day in the hall if she did.

"Um, Miss Amelia, are you going down?" Ray asked, allowing the door to bump against her palm for emphasis.

"I am..." Amelia observed Barker with adoring eyes for a moment longer before she snapped to. "Yes, yes, I am, love. I need to get to the market before too many folks wake up. They're calling for the first snow showers sometime this week, you know? Call it the Southerner in me, but I believe in being prepared." She took the time to nudge Barker with a brush from her shoulder. "Nice to meet you, handsome."

Barker gave a respectful nod. "Thank you, Mrs. Shepard."

"Treat him well, love," Amelia called while the elevator doors slid shut.

Quiet settled following the woman's departure, and then Ray shook her head. "Sorry about that." Laughter colored her voice.

Barker shrugged. "No need. It tends to happen."

Ray's curiosity was at its height, and still she fought to tamp down her questions at least until she was inside the much-needed sanctuary of her home. With a sigh, she hunted for her keys inside the deep pockets of her shawl. As sending Barker Grant on his way then was pretty much out of the question, there was comfort knowing she wouldn't have to search for adequate small talk. Truthfully, that wasn't something she felt she'd need to worry over. After all, conversation between them had flowed quite freely whenever they'd seen each other.

Those times however… Ray knew those times were far removed from this one. This time, they were alone.

She entered her modest yet cozy apartment with an apology on her lips. "I don't have much to offer— haven't done any real shopping since long before the trip."

"You could take a page from Mrs. Shepard's book."

Ray appreciated the tease. "I'd be afraid to now. She wouldn't like knowing I didn't have proper vittles for one of *the* Delano Grants." She heard his chuckle and felt herself brace against something unexpected that stabbed her fiercely.

"No need to put out your best china," Barker said. "I wasn't raised on that side of the family."

"Well, well." Ray pulled off her shawl before going to work on the low-cut boots. "I won't tell Ms. Amelia that some of the Delano Grants don't go for all the royalty stuff."

"My folks didn't want me growing up feeling entitled."

"But you *are* entitled. Your blood makes that so." Ray shrugged as though the idea was unshakable.

"No…not my blood. It was my great-great-grandfather using his good fortune to get other slaves to freedom that did that."

Ray shook her head reverently. Her expression was rapt with awe. "It must feel amazing to come from a background like that."

Barker shrugged. "It might feel even better if more people in my family remembered it instead of the money and opportunity that came later. A lot of my family members make having a family a real headache, you know?"

Ray replied with an apologetic smile. "I wouldn't. You've still got a big family to call your own—a lot of people would love a problem like that." She flipped on two additional lamps that flooded the room in richer shades of gold. It was then that she noticed how much more intense his gaze had become. "Could I get you something?" she offered. "Tea? I've got coffee but no cream."

"I'm good with whatever you're having," he said.

"It might take a while."

"All right."

Ray disappeared into the kitchen to put on the kettle. Moments later, she returned to the living room. "It's freezing in here." She headed for the hearth. "The fireplace is easy to work." She proved it by pressing a button along the side of the mantel. In seconds, the lamp's golden tint was intensified by the firelight's gleam.

"It's not authentic," Ray said while studying the burgeoning flame, "but it'll do in a pinch. You'll be sweltering inside that coat soon," she warned.

Barker was already removing the wool overcoat. "Authentic doesn't always mean better," he said.

"And you're probably in the minority with that kind of thinking."

"You'd be surprised."

Ray treated herself to only a few additional beats of Barker Grant watching. "I should get back to the kitchen." She headed there and stood before the stove while collecting herself and cooling her nerves. She could feel herself being watched soon after. She turned and found Barker in the doorway.

"I'm out of coffee," she said.

"I'm not here for coffee."

Her smile reflected sarcasm. "Yeah, I know." Turning back to the stove, she hastily pulled out mugs from a small cabinet next to it. She stopped when she felt him behind her. He didn't touch her, but Ray felt him just the same—as though his presence radiated like the sun. She turned, and still Barker didn't touch her. Instead, he leaned close to search her eyes with his.

"I came to see that you got home safe because I didn't like the idea of you coming up here alone. I didn't like the thought of you *being* alone."

"I'm not alone, Barker, and I'm not some sad case needing to be pitied."

"I agree, and because you're not is why I'm here." He smiled, shifting a look past her shoulder. "The water's about to boil."

Ray could've cared less. Again, his words held her in a rapt state. She wanted what his eyes promised. She wanted to know if his mouth was as honey-sweet as the voice that resonated beyond it.

"Ray?" He gave a solitary nod then. "The water."

She snapped to. The reminder, paired with the insistent whistle of the silver kettle, was successful in tugging her thoughts out of the inappropriate places they lingered. With a hasty turn toward the stove, she removed the kettle from the glowing orange burner. When she turned back, Barker was gone.

"So, who's the photographer?" Barker was asking just over ten minutes later.

They were back in the living room with mugs of robust black tea in hand. The remote-controlled blaze across from the sofa bathed the room in comforting warmth.

Ray looked to the piece that had caught Barker's eye. It was one of several that featured her in an array of dance poses in genres ranging from ballet to jazz. "Courtesy of Miss Jaz," she said.

Barker smiled, regarding the large photograph above the hearth with renewed interest. "I didn't know she was a photographer." He referred to the late Jazmina Beaumont. The woman had been revered yet scandalized during her reign as one of Philadelphia's most successful female entrepreneurs. Her franchise of gentlemen's clubs had been fixtures across the nation.

Ray snuggled into her side of the long chair she shared with Barker. "She had them professionally done when she was thinking of turning the clubs into dance schools."

Barker showed his surprise. "I thought that was Clarissa's idea." Clarissa David was Jazmina Beaumont's niece and Rayelle's oldest friend.

"Nope." Ray sipped her tea. "Miss J had the idea years before but…well, a woman's gotta make a living. A dance school wasn't where the money was—at least it wasn't there for women like Jazmina Beaumont."

"Ahead of her time," Barker noted.

"Very." Ray used her mug to toast and then set it aside.

"It's a shame." Barker's dark eyes continued to roam the photograph with approval and intrigue. "With you for her spokesmodel, they would've been turning away students at the door."

"Hmph…sometimes, I forget that's even me."

The admission had Barker turning reluctantly from the black-and-white picture. It was a vision with Ray captured in a dark leotard, her shoulder-length hair wrapped around her head in a thick braid with a ringlet of small flowers artistically woven throughout.

"How old were you there?"

She shrugged. "Nineteen or twenty."

"Unbelievable." Barker sent another look above the hearth.

"What?" Ray paused en route to reaching for her mug.

"You could've taken that yesterday."

"Ha! Don't be fooled, Mr. Reporter. The thighs in that picture have changed."

Barker put his mug on the mantel and turned. "I can't tell how that's a bad thing," he said.

Just like that, Ray felt absorbed in the mesmerizing depths of his stare, until he broke the spell.

"So, why don't you recognize yourself?" He smiled, watching as she worked to fix on the question.

Ray noticed and had to wonder if he was purpose-fully trying to keep her off-kilter. If so, he was damn good at it.

"Miss J always thought I could be more than what she thought I was settling for by working for her."

"And what was that?"

"Well, she wanted to be a serious dancer. She thought I did, too. Doesn't everyone?" Ray shifted on the sofa and shrugged. "I mean, who'd want to take her clothes off for money? It wasn't my life's dream, but neither was becoming renowned on the world's stage."

"She wanted more for you."

"She'd already given me more. I was more from the day I met her." Ray blinked, as though suddenly real-izing where she was—what she was saying. She didn't dare look to Barker Grant then. The man was way too easy to talk to. Which was dangerous, considering there were things she'd forbidden herself to ever speak of out-side of certain circles...

Barker didn't pry. "You don't have to be afraid of me, Ray," he told her instead. She looked at him then, stunned. *Good*, he thought. It was the reaction he'd hoped for. He'd known full well that wasn't what she'd been thinking. He knew wherever her thoughts were settled, it wasn't a place she wanted to share with him.

"I've been told I can be intimidating." Barker added a faint shrug as though he considered the idea a ridic-ulous one.

Though she considered herself relatively safe with him, Ray found the notion far from ridiculous. While Barker Grant was considered to be a respected journal-ist both at home and on the national landscape, many believed it was his looks that accounted for much of his "celebrity."

*Fierce* and *intimidating* were natural terms that came to mind when the man was the topic of conversation. Ray had been privy to quite a few of those chats, especially following the recent case that had started with discrepancies in Jazmina Beaumont's own franchise. Those discrepancies had culminated with the takedown of several high-ranking Philadelphia officials—thanks in part to Barker. His station, WPXI, had started putting certain key pieces in place before any real suspicions were ever conjured.

No surprise there—much of Barker's respect stirred from spot-on instincts that had resulted in stories that had toppled big names in Philadelphia and beyond. Intelligence, instincts, to-die-for looks fringed with the unmistakable hint of ferocity and...yes, intimidation was an understandable reaction.

Ray supposed she should've at least felt somewhat unnerved at being alone in her apartment with a man she didn't really know—a man who seemed to fill a room with his presence without saying a word. She supposed she should have considered the possibilities of what could happen if she wanted him to leave and he chose not to...she hadn't considered any of those things. Asking Barker to leave hadn't even registered.

"Do you want me to be intimidated?" she asked, her tone quiet.

"No." He leaned on the wall next to the mantel. "You should ask me to go anyway, though."

Ray refused to blink or even to swallow around the

sudden lump at the back of her throat. "Why would you want me to do that?"

"Because if I stay, we'll be here for a while, and most of that time will be spent doing what we should've been doing in the Bahamas. What we should've been doing long before the Bahamas."

"I'm confused." She said the words while sharing a look that expressed just the opposite. Part of her hoped they would continue along this line of discussion. The other part of her anticipated him changing tactics on her once again.

"That's a shame." He pushed off the wall.

Ray pegged the edge to his soft voice as resignation, and she assumed their time together had reached its end. She stood, deciding to beat him to the door. Instead, she found her path blocked and then she was taken off her feet entirely.

"Where?" he queried against her cheek.

*Anywhere,* the initial response came to mind silently before she reconsidered. She'd stand a better chance of keeping him longer if he were in her bed.

*Desperate, Ray?* a voice jibed. So what if she was? She'd damn well earned the right to treat herself, and what better treat than over six foot five inches of well-defined dark onyx muscle with a stunning brain to match.

"Around the corner—the door at the end of the hall," she said.

"That far, huh? Will you cut me some slack if we make it as far as the hall?"

Laughter bubbled inside Ray's chest, but was stifled by the quick deep lunge of Barker's tongue inside her mouth. She shuddered against him, and Barker felt his sure grip weaken where he cradled her bottom.

He had bargained about making it as far as the hall, but was suddenly weighing the odds of making it from the living room. Rayelle Keats had been a fixture in his mind for too long not to have her presence now wreaking all sorts of chaos on his mind and body. He stood there with her in the middle of the warm, bright room, kissing her like they had all the time in the world. He didn't intend to rush this. He'd meant what he'd said. They'd be there for a while.

# Chapter 2

All Ray wanted was out of her clothes. Well…maybe that wasn't *all* she wanted. It'd be a fine start, though. Anything to bring her a few steps closer to the bliss she had no doubt she'd find in Barker Grant's arms.

He wasn't exactly preventing her from stripping, but her hands felt deliciously weak in the wake of his touch, where they rested in loose fists at his shoulders. His wide palms kneaded her bottom where he cupped it.

The slow massaging strokes were as soothing as those his tongue used to pamper her mouth. When he did withdraw from the kiss, it was to slide his mouth along the line of her neck. His perfect teeth grated the column intermittently as it lowered. Drawing closer to the base of her throat, he used the tip of his tongue to deftly stroke the area until she was all but breathless.

Barker took the path toward the hall that was just past the longest wall in the gold-lit room. By then, his mouth was at her earlobe. He suckled the spot in a way Ray felt captured the perfect blend of pleasure and pain.

Again, she made an effort—a weak one—to get out of her clothes. Her short-waist burgundy-and-emerald knit sweater was easy enough to discard. The cap-sleeved button-down shirt beneath it took a bit of undoing. This was due to Barker trading his captivating suckle at her lobe for driving his tongue into her ear and rotating the tip while she gasped and shuddered anew.

All the while, Barker continued his trek toward the hall. He made terrific progress, though he kept his steps slow. That wasn't only for safety's sake, but more to relish the feel of her body next to his. She was a slender thing, and yet the actual feel of her told a different story. She felt lush and supple as opposed to fragile. Her bottom abundantly filled his wide palms and they cupped, squeezed and fondled to no end. Silently, Barker cursed the fact that she was still inside her jeans. Not for long, he swore.

Ray's arms were linked about his neck, her elegant fingers playing lazily at his nape and the sleek hair tapered there. Her moans carried on a sultry chord that entwined with her frequent gasps, which were the personification of erotic. How had this woman eluded him for so long? Then again, Barker supposed she hadn't. Not really. He'd merely been waiting for the right time. Perhaps they both had.

Ray worked earnestly to rid herself of the shirt Barker had watched her board the plane wearing when they left Nassau. He'd been doing a fine job of not objectifying her during their time down there. At least, he *hoped* he'd done a fine job of not letting on that he'd been objectifying her. That wasn't saying much for him, but what she thought was very important. She had been objectified enough in her life.

Besides, the tropics didn't require much in the way of clothing. Barker wouldn't lie—at least not to himself— that he very much wanted to know what Rayelle Keats looked like out of her clothes—what she was like in bed...

He was about to have those questions answered. *She was a woman a man would want to keep...*those words filtered back to the front of his mind. He'd remembered saying them during a talk with one of his old friends during the trip. Somehow, he knew he'd feel that way once they crossed certain boundaries.

Of course he'd want to keep her. The question would still remain however—would she *want* to be kept?

Ray had managed to free one arm from her puffy shirt sleeve, and Barker decided to help with the rest. They were nearing the end of the corridor. Barker stopped there, putting her between himself and the wall. He used a knee to anchor her there and to free his hands in order to assist.

She'd managed to undo the buttons to just below her bra, enabling her to tug her arm from the sleeve. Barker stopped short of ripping the delicate buttons en route to opening the rest of her shirt. The sight of her generous cleavage heaving above the bra's lacy confines sent heat rising at the collar of his shirt. The garment's front clasp was a welcome sight. With the press of a thumb, he unhooked the fastening with expert skill. His seductively curved mouth was there to capture a nipple when a breast spilled free of the dark lace.

Ray felt weakness infuse her hands again. She could barely cling to his biceps, which felt like long stone slabs beneath her palms. He seemed to devour a pert, pebble-hard bud while his thumb raked its twin with firm, repetitive strokes. Eagerly, she pushed her breast deep into his mouth and emitted a long, shaky moan that captured the hint of a sigh.

Barker wasn't silent either. His groans crested on rough, rugged chords that mimicked the way his tongue handled the nipple it bathed. Once satisfied he'd tended to it properly, he moved on to its mate. So as not to totally abandon the bud, his thumb grazed the wet peak with the same firm strokes.

Ray bit down hard on her lip as though the move enabled her to more intensely savor the unexpected treat. Just as she'd come to accept her relationship with Barker Grant would go no further...this happened. Despite his gifted, attentive manner, she expressed a disappointed whine when he altogether abandoned her chest.

Instead of shushing her, Barker re-engaged their kiss, which proved to be a far more effective silencer. Ray sensed when they'd crossed her bedroom threshold. Silently, she commended the man's talent for following instructions and then figured much of that had to do with his reporter's instincts.

She'd expected to soon feel her bed at her back, but Barker had her meeting another wall instead. Ray had no argument. Her shirt and bra had drifted to the floor long ago—her spot at the wall would give him leave to undo her jeans.

In the spirit of reciprocity, she made a hasty yet efficient effort at sending his shirt to the floor. It didn't take long to bare what she knew—if only by sight—to be a superior chest. Sight had nothing on touch, she discovered when his shirt hit the floor and they met flesh-to-flesh.

She was moving to the waistband of his jeans when Barker set her down suddenly. A few vicious tugs had her denim peeling away from her legs and thighs. Eagerly, she kicked herself free of the material, along with the panties and tights she wore. She had but a moment to bask in the feel of being out of her travel clothes.

Soon, Barker had her positioned in what appeared to be his preferred spot for her against the wall. Ray locked her legs around his back and realized he was as bare as she. He seamlessly freed himself of her hold and she smiled, observing the condom he'd taken from his jeans.

"You came prepared." Her words were slurred.

Barker used his teeth to rip into the packaging. "Hope you're not offended," he said.

"I'll worry about it later—" Her response broke on a gasp when he tugged her closer.

He spread her thighs, yet cupped them loosely in an encompassing grip. With ample space to accommodate his broad frame, he took her body in one filling stroke. Ray's gasps became hiccups flavored with erotic approval. Barker murmured a lurid curse into the dip of her neck as he sank into the deep, moist well of her sex. Faintly, he berated himself for not taking time to more properly ready her. He'd make it up—there was no doubting that. With the plan settled in his mind,

Barker gave himself over to the range of sensation and pleasure rifling through him.

His strength was as impressive as it was arousing, she thought while Barker used one steely arm to support her. His other rested against the wall—forearm lying flush against it. The only sign of weakness he showed was the once clenched fist, now barely closed, against the wall as he gasped harshly into her neck.

Rayelle's gasps then resembled sighs that betrayed the weakest strains of blissful laughter. She felt herself being stretched anew with each thrust he subjected her to. The strokes were deep, long and deliciously intense. When her sighs caught on a hiccup or sharp gasp, that intensity became ruthless, relentless and shockingly infectious.

Between the wall at her back and the wall of muscle trapping her against it, Ray felt suspended between an almost desperate need for release and the need to remain suspended in the lusty wave she rode with eager greed. Barker cradled her bottom in both hands, using the improved stance to drive her in a fiercely erotic manner that all but stole her breath. She kept her arms locked tightly at his neck. She was sensitive enough to feel every square inch of his flesh against hers. Her nipples tingled as they crushed into the unyielding brick that was his chest. She could feel the tips of his middle fingers grazing her folds and keeping time to the potent advance and retreat of his erection staking a sultry claim. She could feel his perfect teeth raking her shoulder and the wildly sensitive spot below her ear.

Delicious as it all was, nothing compared to the sensation of his release flooding her core. She could feel the warmth of it against the condom's thin sheeting. He secured her thighs in a hold that danced the line between firm and viselike.

Spreading her more to adequately welcome his frame also deepened the penetration. Ray almost wept from the pleasure she'd been missing for so long. She felt equal parts loose, limber, taut and desperate, while she wavered at the crest of orgasm. His skin was slick against her fingers, and yet nothing masked the dense muscle packed beneath. She could almost envision the seductive ripple of the sleek ebony as he drove her into the wall without mercy. She welcomed the minor discomfort brought on by his attention. It had been too long and she needed to be reminded.

Barker Grant reminded her for the rest of the night.

He reminded her well into the wee hours of the next morning, as well. She woke to the decadent slide of his velvet mouth across her hips, the small of her back and up the dip of her spine before he repeated the course. Ray snuggled the side of her face deeper into the pillow and luxuriated in the sensation of being so completely worshipped by touch.

Her slight writhing against the mess of coverings gave him just enough room to smooth a hand beneath her hip. He claimed her sex with his middle finger, while his thumb launched a rigorous assault on her clit. Ray sputtered a succession of gasps as she grew more lucid. The assault merely heightened. Barker had two fingers at work inside her then. He took her to the edges of fierce climax and somehow—expertly—refused to let her tip over the treacherous edge.

His mouth had returned to suck and nibble the supple flesh at her hip. His teeth grazed and soothed, making way for his tongue to ease the pleasurably painful ache. The rigor with which his thumb circled her core eased a fraction. The move caused Ray's inner muscles to move viciously to squeeze the invading digits, bathing them in an abundance of her creamy flow as she labored to find her release.

She was whining her approval into a nearby pillow and being slammed by waves of orgasmic overload when she heard the telltale crinkling of condom foil as he ripped into another package. Just how prepared was he? She had wondered more than once that night… day—she'd lost track of the time.

When Barker moved to take her from behind, the swift unapologetic lunge wedged a shocked cry into her whining. He captured her hips, timing her pace to his satisfaction, which was savage and merciless at times, yet delectably smooth and coaxing at others. She never wanted the moment to end.

It didn't, naturally. There were no complaints, not when the enviable length and width of his sex went even more rigid inside her seconds before eruption. Ray came with stunning ferocity, and she could feel her need dampening the twisted sheets beneath them.

Barker followed her down, shielding her slight frame with his broad one as the waves of sexual unrest receded. Again, his hand smoothed down her belly to cup her mound.

"Barker…plea…mmm…" Her lazy words surged when his thumb launched another exploration of her clit and core. She didn't know whether her words were a cry for retreat or continuance.

Barker took them for the latter. Sensing this, Ray accepted that he was offering her only a scant break before he returned for more of her. As time was precious, she closed her eyes in hopes of catching the briefest of naps.

Ray woke later that morning—early afternoon, technically—to the smell of coffee and…scones? Yes… blueberry—her nostrils confirmed it, flaring to take in the fragrance that crowded the room.

Barker, wearing only his jeans slung low on lean hips, knelt near her side of the bed and waved a mug of coffee before her nose. Ray barely cracked open an eye. Her heart lurched, not at the sight of the tall cup emblazoned with the emblem of her preferred diner three doors down, but at the man who presented it.

He was an amazing thing to look at, and part of her couldn't believe he was actually there and…in such a capacity. With a sigh, she set the thought to the back burner of her mind. There'd be plenty of time for that later. Much later.

"You need to eat," he said.

"'Kay" was her sleepy response, but she made no effort to move. "Are we done?" she asked.

Barker didn't answer straight away. He preferred to take his time observing the provocative image she cast lying half in half out of the wrinkled mass of covers. Arousal coursed hot and wickedly at the sight of a long, shapely calf, lush thigh and hint of honey-brown cheek. She'd slept on her stomach, with her arms hidden beneath a pillow and half of her lovely face illuminated by a quiet smile.

"No ma'am," he finally answered. "But I'm gonna need you to eat. Can't have you giving out on me before I'm done with you. Up now, there's food to be had."

The bass carrying his voice accompanied a firm chord that brooked no argument. A bit more lucid then, Ray had no qualms about pushing aside the covers. She got to her knees while reaching for the tall cup. For Rayelle Keats, coffee was life.

She took her first sip of the creamy French roast. No sugar, she noted, thinking of how much of her favorite treat she'd consumed during the trip. God, the man was observant. She relished the hot flood of the beverage through her system and smiled.

Barker had settled against the bottom of a powder-blue Queen Anne chair and simply took in the sight of her.

For Rayelle, it didn't take long for understanding to strike. She felt her cheeks burn and knew it had nothing to do with the temperature of her coffee. She could practically see herself perched on her knees at the edge of the bed, stark naked from a night of very excellent sex and gulping down coffee like a mad woman. When she thought it over, it didn't sound so bad. Then she recalled Barker's dazed expression.

"I'm sorry," she said.

He frowned a little as he smiled. "You'll have to tell me why you feel the need to say so."

Ray shifted to the head of the bed, coffee in one hand, while she used the other to tug at the top sheet. "I'm not used to having company."

"Good."

Her cheeks were on fire then. Nerves were having their way with her, something she rarely, if ever, experienced. "I don't wear a lot of clothes at home." She winced at hearing the first words that came to her mind take flight on her tongue.

"Good," Barker replied. "You won't be needing your clothes for a while."

Ray sipped from her cup and then used it to motion toward Barker. "See, you were kind enough to grab some of yours."

"Some."

He stood then, and Ray forgot all about her divine coffee. He hadn't bothered to secure the button fly, and a slight tug sent the jeans to the floor. He wore nothing beneath.

"Better?" He stepped from the denim.

*Yes,* she answered inside her head. To be honest, the man wore a pair of jeans better than most runway models she'd seen.

"Thanks." She tipped her cup in satisfaction.

Barker moved in to take the cup. "You need to eat." He set the cup to the beige oak dresser on the other side of the chair. "But you won't need much energy for this."

Ray's breath caught in her throat when he shoved her lightly to her back and followed her down. Instead of covering her, he hovered at her waist.

Settling on his stomach, Barker captured her thighs, spreading them to reveal what he'd all but branded with his name during the course of the long, exquisite night they'd shared. Breathing seemed to be a fruitless endeavor when he took her with his tongue. Immediately, her core muscles convulsed around the thrusting organ. She was greedy for the bliss it provided and put her best effort into conquering what he seemed set on withholding. She wanted everything he had to give.

Unfortunately, Barker wasn't in the mood to allow it. Ray's fingers threaded through his thick, gossamer-soft hair in an attempt to tug him deeper, enough to shove her over the line into sublime elation. Alas, Barker wasn't in any hurry. Hands vise-tight on her thighs, he kept her anchored to the bed and open to a slow, tormenting exploration of her sex. His scent all over her body was an aphrodisiac of the highest caliber. He could've breathed in her fragrance for the rest of the day and night.

The way she moved in his hands, reacting with the fiercely feminine sounds of desire and satisfaction… she was going to make it impossible for him to walk away. *Idiot*, he thought while feverishly drinking her in. He'd known there'd be no walking away since long before he walked into her apartment the previous day. She was a woman no man could walk away from once he'd had her.

He had no intention of letting this end. The question was how to get her intentions to align with his. Sex? Barker rotated his tongue deep, languidly, and felt a new rush of her intimate moisture begin to coat his taste buds as her fingers weakened in his hair.

No, sex wasn't the way…but oh, what a side benefit it was. He'd need that benefit, as he suspected the beauty, who was ordering him not to stop, believed she'd never see him again once he'd had his fill.

Oh, yes, he was going to enjoy changing her mind.

# Chapter 3

They woke the next morning tucked in each other's arms on the sofa, where they'd cuddled after yet another exhaustive and illicit romp the night before.

The romp had started in the shower, continued in the bedroom and resumed halfway to the kitchen. Sleep arrived as subtle as a thousand-pound weight. Barker and Rayelle crashed on the sofa following a late-night snack of ginger ale and Pop-Tarts.

Ray woke feeling well-rested instead of panicked or embarrassed. She'd held nothing back with Barker Grant—a man she didn't know well before—a man she *still* didn't know. They hadn't exactly spent all their time together talking. In their defense, they'd spent enough time talking in the Bahamas and during the many months prior to that, just after his best friend had started a relationship with hers. Given that, Ray supposed they'd put in enough talking time to warrant all the other things they'd done for the past forty-eight hours. And yet…she still wasn't sure that it was.

Barker was waking then, following a lazy stretch. He put a kiss to Ray's head and stood, taking her with him by way of slinging her over his shoulder.

"We were on our way to the kitchen before we got sidetracked last night." She slapped at his shoulders. "Scones and Pop-Tarts don't exactly qualify as a filling meal."

Barker's long strides slowed and then stopped altogether as he grunted a curse. He bowed his head as if to consider her argument. The consideration was fleeting, however, and he continued on to the bedroom.

Ray laughed. "This isn't the way to the kitchen!"

"Remind me of what exactly you have in your kitchen besides end pieces of bread, four Saltines and less than half a liter of ginger ale?"

"There's my box of Earl Grey," she said.

"Right." His tone was flat.

Barker deposited Ray on the center of her bed when they entered the room. Leaving her there, he took his phone from the bureau, where he'd left it after returning from the diner for scones the day before.

Ray waited, tucking her legs beneath her. Gone was her self-consciousness over parading naked around her home before him. The way Barker's bottomless gaze followed her was a decadence she didn't mind savoring. She tuned in to his phone conversation then. Intrigue pooled in her almond-toned eyes when she realized he was ordering groceries. He wrapped up the call, having instructed whomever was on the other end to "charge his account." Ray's jaw dropped thoroughly. Her gaze, however, was level with her voice when she spoke.

"You don't have to buy me groceries."

"I know that." Barker set aside the phone and returned to the bed, where he sat opposite her. Leaning close, he planted a fist on either side of her hips.

"I'm not trying to buy you, Ray, but I'm not a fun person to be around when I'm hungry."

Her heart flipped over the slow, adorable smile that emerged, but her head was stuck on his prior comment. "I don't think you're trying to buy me, Barker."

"I don't see how that's possible." He posed the argument softly. "I bet all I own that men try it all the time."

They did. In the world of exotic dance and gentlemen's clubs, such things were common. "I should say that no one's ever tried it with groceries."

A touch of Barker's innate playfulness entered his tone. "You're going to have to recognize when a man's being a jackass and when he's being considerate."

"I'll work on it."

Satisfied, he rolled a broad, dark shoulder. "See that you do."

"Will you at least let me thank you for it?"

He gave a full shrug then. "That's allowed."

"Thank you." She scooted closer. "Will you let me thank you with a kiss?"

Barker grinned. "That's always allowed."

The groceries arrived before lunchtime. Barker and Rayelle were both showered and presentable to receive the order, which consisted of twelve expertly yet densely packed plastic bags. Instead of having the generously tipped delivery driver carry them up, Barker and Rayelle handled that part of the job themselves.

"I won't have to shop for at least a month," Ray marveled as they stepped from the elevator.

Once again, they met up with the outspoken Amelia Shepard.

"I'm glad to see Miss Ray is treating you well," she said to Barker.

"I needed groceries anyway, Miss Amelia."

"Mmm-hmm… I'm not just talking about the groceries, love."

Silence carried for several beats following the woman's departure.

"So how thick are your walls?" Barker asked.

"No idea." Ray grimaced. "If it hasn't happened already, by morning it'll be all over the building that we spent the weekend together."

"I can live with that." Barker sent her a wink. "A weekend with you will send my stock through the roof."

"Good to know, since I already planned to tell Miss Amelia we're only friends. That still wouldn't have worked out well for you, though. She would've just asked for my help trying to set you up with one of her nieces."

"That bad, huh?"

"That good," Ray corrected. "They're beautiful, but married to men Miss Amelia hates."

Laughter carried from the corridor as Barker and Ray carted the groceries inside the apartment. Barker dutifully unpacked the items and left them on the kitchen table while Ray did the same with the packages on the counter.

"It'll only take a few minutes to put everything away, and then it's all yours," she called over her shoulder.

Barker had already volunteered to fix lunch. Ray worked diligently at the counter for several minutes. She was putting a box of macaroni into a top cabinet when she felt his hand at her waist.

"Lunch, Barker," she reminded him once he'd undone the button of her jeans and was at work on the zipper. She placed the pasta on its shelf and had another box in hand ready to place alongside it. Her hand suddenly weakened on the box and would've taken a tumble were it not for Barker's expert catch. His other hand never once wavered from her jeans.

"Bar—"

"Shh... I'm only checking to see if you kept to the agreement."

"You know I did." Her words were breathless. "You watched me dress, didn't you?"

The "agreement" had been clothes only—no underwear.

"A good reporter always checks," Barker murmured. His mouth brushed Ray's neck and made its way up to suck her double-pierced lobe, bereft of earrings just then.

Ray saw no point in arguing with his reasoning. She couldn't have argued anyway. She doubted her brain was capable of allowing much in the way of speech.

"See?" she managed once his hand slid into her open jeans and his thumb brushed the bare mound of flesh above her sex.

"Good girl," he said and then, as if to reward her for

keeping her word, lowered his thumb to lightly work her clit.

Ray let her head fall back, mouth open to emit a throaty wail. The sound caught, incapable of total escape when his middle finger joined in with the sensual torture as he took thorough possession of her sex. The long, thick digit slid high and brought Ray to the tips of her sneakers in reaction to surging ecstasy. She tried to reach up and back, wanting to lose her fingers in the ebony crop of his soft hair. But her hands seemed capable only of clutching the doors of the open cabinet she faced.

Barker feasted on Ray's ear as if the lobe gave him nourishment. He supposed it did—just as the relentless squeeze and release of her inner muscles working overtime around his finger turned the digit slick with her need. Mercilessly, he pushed her further. His fingers skirted the hem of the lavender Henley she wore before they disappeared beneath.

Ray flinched when she felt him there.

"Shh…" he urged again. "Gotta check it all."

She could only reply with a brief quaking moan when his hand closed over a bare breast. His thumb started to flick across a hard nipple, and her core worked with greater intensity around his invading finger. She shattered when he tugged at the nub before he pinched it. She gulped a great amount of air as her climax slammed into her. Residual shudders lasted for long moments once the orgasm began to ebb.

Barker eased the intensity of the potent strokes he'd been subjecting Ray to. Gradually, his fingers stilled and then withdrew. She eased her desperate grip on the cabinet doors, trading it for one at the edge of the chrome sink. She remained there until her breathing bore some resemblance to its normal pace.

Barker kept a steadying hand at her waist once his other slipped from beneath her top. He dropped a quiet kiss to her ear and squeezed her hip again.

"Come to bed when you're done here."

The pat he gave her bottom was more of a squeeze and had Ray steeling herself against it as desire returned on an impossibly strong wave.

Lunch never materialized, but Barker made up for that by putting together an incredible dinner. By then, Ray had sobered somewhat. Part of her mind—her body—was still in her bedroom and being supremely pleasured by the dark, powerful male who'd had command of her for over forty-eight hours. She picked up her fork and set it back to her plate for a third time.

Barker had no trouble massacring the gargantuan rib eye he'd prepared. "Hungry?" he asked her.

"Starved."

"I get it," he said, grinning. "Not used to anyone cooking in your apartment except you."

Ray recognized his dig about her not entertaining company much. "I'll have you know I actually have the luxury of quite a few people taking over my kitchen from time to time."

That got more of Barker's attention, pulling it from the perfectly cooked steak. "If you won't eat, could you at least share some details?"

"Nothing too secretive. Clari's over a lot, so are the

girls from the club, and then there are my girls from the center so…"

The last captured more of Barker's attention.

"I volunteer at a local home for teen girls." She hesitated over the slice of steak she'd forked up. "Haven't done as good a job as I should be doing with the clubs changing over to schools."

"I didn't know that."

"Oh, yeah." Ray savored her cut of steak. "We're in the process of changing over the clubs—"

"No, I mean your volunteer work." He sat back in his chair, watching her with mounting admiration. "How long?"

"Since I moved here from Miami, actually."

"Impressive." He practically sighed the word. "You've been here since your teens. That's some dedication, Ray. Few people manage to stick to volunteer commitments unless they're required to."

"Yeah." Ray enjoyed another bite of the tender meat. "I really wanted to do it, especially back then. I didn't want anyone making the kinds of mistakes I did, or was about to."

"Not a very positive outlook on that time."

"I was a teenager back then. Besides—" she set down her fork once more "—I came here knowing mistakes would be required if I planned on getting what I wanted."

"And that was?"

"To make it on my terms," she replied without hesitation. "I didn't want to explain how I did it or why I did it the way I did."

"Bold. Dangerous," Barker noted.

Ray enjoyed her steak with a little more gusto then. "Most *bold* things are."

"Luck has to play a role, too, right? Young girl trying to make it on her own here. Most don't live to tell a tale like that."

"You're right, but I had something better than luck—Jaz Beaumont."

Barker grinned while conjuring an image of the bodacious woman who was responsible for a fair amount of the scandalous news in Philadelphia during her time.

"Your best friend's aunt was quite a woman."

"She was that." Ray smiled, remembering. "She always said living life to the fullest often meant getting yourself snared in a fair amount of scandal."

"Guess that's true. I wouldn't have had much of a career if it wasn't."

"Shouldn't you sound a little happier about it?" Ray regarded her dinner partner curiously.

"And that's the misconception. A reporter's job is to share info—not to revel in the fact that the info could be rewarded if it's dark enough."

Ray gave a subtle shake of her head. "You're not the average reporter."

"Maybe I am—seems I've been sharing a lot of dark news lately and getting rewarded for it."

"Ah—your pending promotion. I remember you mentioning it in the Bahamas. Any closer to making a decision whether to accept?"

Barker fiddled with his silverware. His expression was a smidge brooding. "Accepting would give me more power over future stories. Whether or not they see the light of day, that kind of thing."

"But?"

Barker smiled, appreciating her perception. "It might put a current story in jeopardy."

"Because you're still not willing to give your staff the freedom to take the reins? I remember you saying something about that, too."

Barker shifted, getting a little more comfortable in his seat. "I think they'd do fine. It's the dancing around those who'd prefer they didn't that I worry about them handling."

"I see." Ray bathed a sliver of steak in the special sauce Barker had made. "Always the never-ending tug of war between the worker bees and management. I'd think one of the revered Grants could find ways around that."

"I could, if I was willing to trade on my name and money. I'm not—I can't. If I did, I'd never know if that power was due to my strength as a writer or something else."

"Barker, Barker…has anyone ever told you you're too honorable for your own job—I mean, your own good?"

He chuckled, noting the dig. "It's why I'm suspicious of accepting this new opportunity."

"You really think they'd do that? Offer you one job to keep you from doing another?"

"It'd be very stupid and desperate of them if they did." Barker finished the beer he'd had with his dinner. "Desperate because it means they've got something to hide. Stupid because they've told me so. They know I'm thinking about the offer at least. That buys me some time to figure out the rest, I guess."

"And what if you don't find anything else?"

"That's the other misconception, Ms. Keats." Barker leaned in to finish his meal. "There's always something to find—always another layer to the story. At least there is when you start to uncover information. That's the level I'd like to reach—the one that leads to the end of the story."

"Where everyone lives happily-ever-after?"

"That's what they tell me." Barker studied Rayelle closely. "Why do I get the impression you're interested in all this for a more personal reason?"

"Always more to the story, huh?" Ray said.

Barker shrugged. "You're just easy to read."

She laughed. "Most don't think so."

"Most don't know you."

Ray decided against following up on the comment. "All don't live happily-ever-after, you know? There's always someone left out in the cold. No one gets everything they want out of the mix."

"And since that group tends to include the bad guys, no one cares much."

"Bad guys aren't always involved, Barker, just people trying to do the right thing without realizing it could put others in a bad place."

"You're not on board with Clarissa's changes to her aunt's club, are you?"

Ray felt her heart lurch over the sudden shift in topic. Yes, he was good. Instead of verbal confirmation to his probe, she merely stared.

"I know how to keep my mouth shut, Ray."

She gave a weary shake of her head. "It's no secret. Clari knows I've got reservations."

"Does she know how strong they are?"

The query had Ray leaving the table.

"How long before you tell her?"

"Never," Ray responded quickly. "This is what Miss J always wanted."

"What she wanted, but was hesitant to act on," Barker mused.

"It had nothing to do with money." Ray came swiftly to her late mentor's defense. "Miss J knew her clubs— the girls she employed…she knew it was all they had. She gave them a way when there wasn't one—not one that wouldn't have them doing things that could eventually put their lives in jeopardy, at any rate."

Ray went to stand before the hearth where the flames burned low. "She understood that her dreams weren't everyone else's, and she was big enough to step back from them to give her people what they needed. She could've gotten out of the gentlemen's club business and into something more *respectable* a long time ago—shutting up everyone who tried to judge her. She wouldn't let what others thought rule her actions."

"You loved her a lot, didn't you?"

Ray nodded eagerly. "Clari did, too, but…well…she was gone during so much of what Miss J went through. She sees her aunt's dream as a testament to her life, but those girls—their happiness—*that* was the testament."

"Will you tell Clarissa that?"

"I would if I knew how."

"You think Clarissa would resent you for it?"

"I think I'd resent myself for it. If Clari holds back from changing things, those girls might never have the chance to know if they could be more than a piece of meat for some guy to drool over."

"In the end, it's their choice, you know?" Barker kept his voice soft. "Jazmina Beaumont ran her business with its own set of limits, and there were those who tested those limits, remember?"

"Yeah." Ray rested a fist along the mantel. "Yeah, I remember." She drew her hands through her hair then. "I don't consider a choice between a stripper and a ballerina an easy one—even a realistic one," she said. "Knowing how to do something isn't a guarantee of being paid to do it." She smiled then, feeling Barker's arms sliding around her waist.

"Don't be so hard on yourself." He spoke into her neck.

She laughed. "Are you about to tell me that's your job?"

Barker laughed then, too. "I wasn't going to, but now that you mentioned it…" He began to tend the satiny flesh at her nape.

Ray was poised to let herself be tugged under a wave of sensation, but he stopped.

"I think you could come up with a plan to give everybody their happily-ever-after."

Ray felt wary over the possibility he proposed. "You've got a lot of faith in me, but I'm not the creative thinker you might believe."

Barker held her tighter. "I believe quite a bit when it comes to how creative a thinker you are."

"Sounds like I've got you fooled."

"Convinced is more like it. Shall I show you why?"

Ray was eager to take her mind off anything remotely confrontational. She was eager for just a few more hours with the man drawing her into his arms.

"I'd like that," she said. "I'd like that a lot."

# *Chapter 4*

*Three days later*

Ray scanned the pad with a cool look and wasn't surprised to find that it offered no hints about the topic currently under discussion. That would've been impossible, of course, considering she'd done little more in the way of note-taking, except to draw a series of squiggly lines and circles of varying sizes between the margins of a yellow legal pad.

Nevertheless, she took time to refer to the page, if only to treat herself to a few additional seconds before experiencing the inevitable embarrassment of meeting the inquiring eyes of her staff and business partner.

Clarissa David cleared her throat and stood to address the group of women occupying the cozy office.

"You'll hear from us—" she sent a smile down the table toward Ray "—when we know more about the contractor's proposed dates. We'll discuss how to deal with the current clientele at that time. Until then, start thinking of new ideas to make the transition easier."

Clarissa took a few final questions and then adjourned the meeting.

"In case you're wondering about the question that was on the table before you zoned out," Clarissa said once she and Rayelle were alone, "it was whether or not we're to tell prospective employees about our plans for the school."

"Right." Ray nodded. "Thanks for the save. Guess that answer rests on whether we're still keeping it a secret that changing over to schools is the plan for all the clubs."

"Guess that all depends on you."

Ray's zoned-out expression cleared abruptly. "Me?"

Clarissa looked as though she was hard at work trying to shield a smile. "Where's your head, Ray? I guess you forgot you haven't given me an official yes about taking over out here."

"Taking over." Ray felt newly dazed.

"Well, Ray, I've got responsibilities for Aunt Jaz's businesses out west—it'll be hard giving my all to the ones here without your help. If that help can't come from you, it's gonna have to be someone."

"Right, right." Ray hid her face in her hands then. She had completely blanked on that part in the latest round of negotiations regarding the Jazzy B's franchise.

Declining Clarissa's offer would be one way to stave off having to discuss her disagreement with the majority of those changes. Unfortunately, declining Clarissa's offer would also have the woman demanding to know why. Ray figured she could always lie and tell Clarissa that she was just too exhausted to take on a job like that…but she owed her friend the truth.

A thunderous commotion sent Ray's thoughts back to the present, and she saw that Clarissa had intentionally slammed down a bookend that supported a broad stack of folders. The woman's expression all but screamed her concern.

"I'm sorry, Clari—"

"Save it. I don't want your apologies, I want to know what the hell's going on with you."

Ray tugged her hair free of its low ponytail and pulled a hand through her messy locks. "Guess I'm still lagging after the trip—an amazing trip, but I'm beat."

"Understandable." Clarissa eased into her chair at the round table in the Jazzy B's manager's wing, where they'd met with the employees. A sly smile took shape on her mouth. "I would've thought you'd have had more fun once we got back over the weekend."

Ray frowned, waiting for her friend to clarify.

Clarissa seemed to relish her words. "I'm sure I wasn't the only one who noticed how Barker insisted on seeing you home when we landed."

"He didn't insist." Ray dropped her eyes to the table. Once again, she searched for solace among the series of squiggly lines and circles doodled on the legal pad.

"Oh, he insisted all right," Clarissa argued coolly. "The least you can do is soothe my curiosity with a tiny explanation. I don't need *all* the details unless you just *want* to share—which wouldn't be strange considering we're best friends and all."

"Clari, look, I—" Ray was about to say there were no details, but she couldn't complete the lie.

Clarissa's eyes widened in tandem with her mouth curving into a perfect O-shape. Seconds later, she was using both hands to cover it. "Barker Grant is a man who knows how to take his time," she said finally.

"Amen to that," Ray mumbled.

"My guess is he knows how to use his time well," Clarissa said. "I've been trying to call you all weekend. Do I take that to mean he kept you…indisposed for two days?"

Ray decided she'd go even crazier trying to keep the truth from Clarissa. "It was more like three days," she confessed. "He…um…he didn't leave my place until Monday morning."

Clarissa's eyes went impossibly wider. Instead of her mouth forming an O-shape again, she shrieked delightedly. "He's a man who knows how to make up for lost time." Her sly look returned. "Am I right?"

Ray pushed back from the round table. "You're right. Very."

Clarissa's gaze followed Ray as she took a turn around the room. "So…um…where do things stand with you two?"

"They stand exactly where they stood before and during the Bahamas, Clari. We're friends."

"Ray!"

"All right, *close* friends."

Clarissa looked as though she'd lost the ability to do

more than gawk incredulously. Meanwhile Ray continued to pace the back room.

"Do you really think an entire weekend with him
was just about sex?" Clarissa finally managed to ask.

"I do, Clari, because that's what it is. We're two
grown, mature people who enjoyed something we both
needed, and that was that."

Clarissa snorted. "I'm pretty sure Barker Grant isn't
a man who's hurting for a robust sex life. He seems
smarter than to compromise friendship with sex."

"Grown and mature, Clari," Ray sang, "and male.
If opportunity is there, a man will always choose the
complication if it gets him sex."

"So that's where you left things?" Clarissa countered. "A one-weekend stand—friendship still intact?"

Ray only shrugged.

"And your zoned-out demeanor?"

"Jet lag."

"That's crap. Have you talked to him since—"

"I haven't."

"It's been three days, Ray."

"Friends don't chat every day, Clari. Not even the
close ones."

Clarissa observed her friend with all the knowledge
of one who'd known another for much of their lives.
"Have you not talked to him because he hasn't called,
or because you haven't *taken* his calls?"

"Don't do this, Clarissa." Ray rolled her eyes.

"I'm right." Clarissa was unsympathetic. "Seriously,
Ray?"

"Clarissa, don't."

"Can I at least ask why?" Clarissa insisted.

"He's Barker Grant." Ray seemed to drop what remained of her nonchalant facade then. "He's Barker Grant," she repeated, as though it were all that needed to be said.

"That explains nothing," Clarissa retorted.

"Clarissa, why are you doing this?" Ray groaned, dragging both hands down her face. "I mean, is this how you repay all the understanding I showed when you found Eli?"

"Understanding, huh? You mean the hard time you gave me about him, right? Don't try changing the subject."

"Whatever." Ray threw out a wave. "It's not my fault you can't focus once the guy's name is mentioned." Ray referred to Elias Joss, Clarissa's significant other of almost a year.

"Come on, Ray. What does 'he's Barker Grant' mean?"

Ray faced her friend then. "It means the man's got way too much going on to start an involvement like the one you're speculating over."

"All right, I'll give you that, but why do I get the sense that's not what you really mean?"

"Hell, Clari, give me a break, okay?" Ray resumed her walk around the office. "Respected, award-winning journalist who also happens to be an heir to family wealth that goes back to Civil War times falls in love with an exotic-dancer-turned-dance-studio-manager? Right."

Clarissa blinked as she heard the pain in the voice of her oldest friend. "I'd say that makes Barker Grant a lucky guy."

"Don't patronize me, Clari."

"I wouldn't do that and you know it. This is truth."

"As *you* see it."

"And you don't?"

"I doubt that would matter."

"To who? Barker? Because it sounds like he feels the same as I do."

It was Ray's turn to snort then. "Barker's respectability would fly right out the window if he started something with me."

"Because you manage a dance school." Clarissa made her point drily and overlooked the face Ray made in return. "But technically you're not a dance-school manager since you haven't accepted my offer. And you're no exotic dancer, either. That hasn't been you since what? Twenty-one, twenty-two? You're a long way from those days, hon." She gave her friend a casually measured look.

Again, Ray snorted. "Thanks."

Clarissa shrugged. "Anytime. You manage a respected club, Ray, and have a respected name of your own. *That's* the woman Barker Grant met, the one he started a friendship with—took it to the next level with."

Ray had no comeback, so Clarissa opted to end her argument there. She stood up, crossed over to Ray and pulled her into a hug. "I'm sorry, all right?"

Ray eased back from the embrace. "Sorry?"

"For being so pushy with this. Guess I'm just out of my mind happy, and I want everyone else as happy as I am."

"I get it, Clari." Understanding bloomed in Ray's eyes. "I see how Elias Joss affects you, and I'm pretty sure we'll be attending yet another wedding sometime soon. I haven't even unpacked yet because I know we'll all be heading to sunny skies in the near future."

Clarissa was already shaking her head. "It's too soon for that. It's barely been a year," she insisted at Ray's dubious look. "It's way too soon for us to be talking marriage."

"Says who?"

"Ray…it's just not the way things are done."

"Ah…so there *are* some absolutes in your happy world?" Ray wagged an index finger. "That means I'm allowed to have at least one. A man like Barker Grant doesn't throw over his entire life for—" She stopped at Clarissa's warning look. "For a nightclub manager," she finished.

Clarissa looked totally flummoxed. "I give up."

"All I ask."

"I give up until Barker proves me right."

Ray rolled her eyes and kept them shut even when Clarissa put a kiss to her cheek.

"Get back to me soon, all right? I need to confirm you as manager…or not." Clarissa squeezed Ray's arm, waited for their eyes to meet. "Or not is just fine, too. You know that, right?"

"I know, Clari. It's just a big step, you know? If I'm gonna do this, I need to be sure I'm doing right by Miss Jaz."

"I get it." Clarissa pulled Ray into another hug. "I'll get out of your hair. Think about what I said about Barker, okay? At least admit to yourself that you deserve happiness same as the rest of us."

Ray put a kiss to Clarissa's cheek and forehead. "You don't have to worry over me like that. I'm not stress-

ing out over some old drama that's making me feel un-
worthy, trust me."

"I know." Clarissa gave a quick, tight smile but stifled any additional comment.

Ray watched Clarissa leave. Alone then, she made
a stab at gathering the papers that had spilled from the
folder. Quickly losing interest in the task, she settled
to the edge of the desk and hissed a curse.

"Why now?" Barker was the image of a content soul
as he swiveled the chair at the end of the long rectangular conference-room table.

WPXI programming executives Willard Harold
and Garrett Cole occupied seats at the other end of the
table. Willard Harold began to chortle, which caused
his slightly jowled chin to quiver.

"I'll never figure you out, Grant," he said. "We're
giving you the keys—"

"Keys you've damn well earned, by the way." Garrett Cole's blue-gray eyes held their usual chill, but sin-
cerity lurked just the same.

"Right," Harold confirmed.

"But you want me to stop earning it now, is that
right?"

"We want you to take on something more," Cole
argued.

"Finally." Harold's jowls shook once more as he
pulled a hand through his thinning dark blond hair.

"And what I've got here now? What about that?"
Barker's tone was easy, his deep stare unwavering…
and aware.

"You've been so thorough, the copy could practically

write itself." Cole pointed toward the conference-room door. "With your team on it, putting this thing to bed should be a piece of cake."

Except it wouldn't be. Barker knew that and was well aware that his colleagues knew the same. Of course his staff was well-trained—*he'd* trained them. Still, they had precious little time on the job. They were getting experience and had already cut their teeth on some pretty rigorous features, but they still had no idea how the other side of the game was played.

The office politick back and forth would eat them alive. Barker knew Harold and Cole well enough to see behind the smokescreens. The thing was, they hadn't made seeing behind it difficult at all. That told Barker they were desperate—so much so, they'd gotten sloppy. It also told him that what he'd uncovered to that point was enough to move forward with the story. He had enough to let the public know properties in the city's least affluent areas were being bought at five times their worth. He was on the heels of uncovering the *who*, but he still needed to know the *why*.

His old colleagues were most likely caught up in their own share of the politick, as well. Chances were high they were being strong-armed to pull out every stop at getting Barker to drop the story. Why? Perhaps what he was on to reached people who would prefer this story go away. If it couldn't be dropped, it could damn well be buried. Leaving it all in the hands of an eager-to-please crew might be the perfect way to accomplish that.

He hated to conceive that the crew he'd taken under his wing would ever shrug off all they'd learned and allow themselves to be pulled off the hunt of a cover-up. As he looked down the table at the two well-seasoned news vets, however, he knew that pressure—applied just right and by the right entities—could unsteady the most learned and determined.

Regardless of his suspicions, Barker couldn't totally cast aside Harold and Cole's offer. The spot on the programming board was one that could've been his years ago if he hadn't been so steeped in the grittier side of his job.

In the ivory tower of the programming boardroom, he could be more certain that the stories needing to be told would be. As one of the powers that be, he'd have the authority to determine what WPXI showed its viewing public. Sadly, he wouldn't be in as much of a position to contribute to that potential viewing pool. Saying goodbye to that aspect of the job wouldn't be such a hardship given the devotion he'd shown to his career over the last several years. He'd given enough of himself and supposed *that* outlook had a lot to do with where he'd spent his weekend.

The sex had been superior and the reason his sleep had been piss-poor over the last three nights. Superior sex, however, wasn't all that had kept him so happily ensconced in Rayelle Keats's domain. Knowing what it was like to sleep with and awaken next to the same woman was a pleasure he'd never really afforded himself—not the way he had with Ray.

He was sure that because they'd been working on a real friendship, it played heavily into the allure of the situation, as well. He'd almost been able to gain a sense of what had consumed all of his closest friends in the world. Almost. He wasn't naive enough to believe that a few nights of excellent sex was the foundation for lifelong devotion.

He wasn't about to walk away, though. Part of him knew Ray would think sex was the reason why. Given what he knew of her life, he supposed that was to be expected. He wasn't going anywhere, though, and with that settled, there was only one thing left—getting her plans to align with his. Again, Barker found himself preoccupied with the varied and satisfying ways for making that happen.

Barker's preoccupation didn't last long when he remembered his co-workers seated at the other end of the table.

"So? Why now?" He restated his question. "Over the years, you two have done everything to stifle coverage of almost all my stories. Now you want to reward me for them? Why? And why *now*?"

"Dammit, Grant, we already told you why—"

"Will you make us beg?" Cole interrupted his partner.

"Beg? Why would you do that? Exactly who is this offer coming from?" Barker felt close to laughter. "Contrary to what the two of you might believe, I'm not egotistical enough to think you've finally seen the light. That you're ready to acknowledge my flair and excellence in the world of journalism with a seat of power on a board *you're* not even a part of."

The executives both grimaced over that.

"You know the game as well as we do, Barker," Harold spat. "In the end, affluence always wins. The privileged get what they want no matter how well others play."

"So this generous offer isn't coming from you two after all. What a surprise. Could it be from whoever's pulling your strings to get me to back off of finding out who's buying this property and why?"

"Hell, Barker, everything isn't a cover-up!" Cole raged. "There's no one behind the scenes running an agenda at every turn—"

"Only most of the turns," Barker pointed out, still maddeningly calm. Silently, he thanked Rayelle. True, his easy manner could've been due to the sun and relaxation of the Bahamas. He knew he owed the abundance of his stress relief, however, to Rayelle Keats. Had this "chat" occurred a month ago, he would've already been on his feet and seriously considering upending the table he sat so calmly behind.

"Accept our offer or don't, Grant." Harold seemed to be drawing on a measure of calm, as well. "If you're curious about where the offer came from, try the station owners. They don't want to lose you for obvious reasons."

"Look Barker," Cole chimed in, "no matter our personal issues with each other, you're one helluva reporter. If we can't have you out there uncovering well-buried leads, we at least want you in the fold."

"Is there some question about the way I've been uncovering my leads?" Barker straightened in his chair, intrigue all but crushing him then. "Is my job in danger?"

The executives laughed.

"Far from it!" Cole cried. "You're the best on our

staff. The on-air team would lose their minds without you to depend on."

"Even still, Barker," Harold interjected. "No one could fault you for walking away in light of things."

Barker's sleek brows knit. "In light of what things?"

Harold and Cole traded looks.

"Barker, we've heard about the threats." Cole winced amid the confession. "Minor ones, but it doesn't take much for stuff like this to escalate."

"And we all know it's not the first time I've been threatened."

"But it's the first time others have noticed it taking a toll." The hint of a smile crossed Harold's face when he saw Barker bristle.

Garrett Cole appeared to have noticed Barker's reaction, as well. "Think on it, Barker. That's all we ask."

Following another exchange of looks, the duo stood and left the room. Barker remained. After a while, he reached for the phone and told the person who answered that they needed to talk.

# *Chapter 5*

Endeavor House was a teen girls' center and group home not far from the downtown area. The remodeled old Victorian house was grand in size and impression, and struck its visitors with a sense of reverence for history and purpose. It was a good thing since many of its visitors were young and uncertain, with little regard for their history and no clue of their purpose.

The Endeavor House mission was to give a sense of both. As for purpose, that was what its staff hoped to most greatly instill among the young charges. Ray considered the Endeavor House mission part of a more personal goal. Fourteen years ago, she'd arrived in Philadelphia from Miami. She was a kid herself, very much like the ones who frequented the home.

She'd been a girl full of attitude and self-presumed

wisdom, whose rough upbringing had taken her down a series of rocky roads. This, until fate cut her a break and landed her in the world of a powerful woman with a good heart and a determination to change her path.

Jazmina Beaumont had been Rayelle's Endeavor House, and Ray was now indebted to pay that goodness forward. It was a debt she was happy to repay. Her life could've turned down a truly grotesque path had Jaz Beaumont not seen her as more than a young girl content with spending her life on display for the pleasure of those who could've cared less about her well-being.

While her first step upon arrival in Philadelphia had been Jazzy B's, it didn't take Ray long to scope out others among the young and wayward. She found teen shelters—not like Endeavor House—but places where girls like her had lost their way. She'd gone into those places not to have a roof over her head—Jaz Beaumont had seen to that. She had gone so she wouldn't forget.

Haunted by her past, Ray knew that pretending it never existed, that she'd never been affected by it, made the odds that much greater that her past could once again become her present. When her life began to take shape, growing in definition and purpose, she decided it was time to do more than sit and observe others.

She had walked through the doors of Endeavor House determined to make a difference. She'd volunteered there for just over ten years and had gotten so good at what she did there, the staff had made a flurry of offers in hopes of luring her away from Jaz Beaumont. Ray had declined, but accepted the offer to mentor. Her most recent group included a small, yet decidedly driven group of young women. Ray had sensed an immediate kinship among the circle of four. They looked at Endeavor House not as a destination, but a place to begin again.

Ray knew some of their histories, but not all. It was clear to her that the girls were determined to make their own way in the world, but drew the line at doing that in ways that might be hard or impossible to come back from.

She'd arrived that afternoon with a stash of goodies from the Bahamas. The twenty-five women of the Endeavor House staff adored every item Ray brought in: packets of coffees, teas, island jewelry and hats. For her group of mentees, she'd put together a slideshow that would be shown to them first. The presentation was saved to a drive so that the vivid shots could be shared with the other residents. Ray was excited to get the show underway, eager to see the light of hope and possibility in her group's eyes.

When she made it into the cozy staff lounge, however, she found that she was one mentee short.

"That damn job of hers." Leona Best blew out a laugh. "That's why Suze isn't here."

"Well, it's good to know she's working," Ray said, referring to Suzanne Jessup. "Don't worry, she can watch the show with the others when she gets back."

"Oh, she's not at work, Ray." Bettina Franks spoke up. "She's upstairs, sleeping."

"That's why we're all so peeved about it," Leona said. "The place has her working like a slave 'til all sorts of hours."

"This morning she didn't get here until six thirty," Ajani Pinkney added. "How's she supposed to make it through school with hours like that? She lucked out that today's a teacher workday."

"Those are the breaks, ladies." Ray gave them a crooked smile. "At least she's keeping high school on the plate. Without that diploma, you're at the mercy of whatever job you can get. You guys wanna make it on your own terms? Start by finishing your educations."

Ajani groaned. "Prepare yourselves, guys, it's another college chat."

"No, that way isn't for everyone." Ray clicked on the drive's icon. "There are lots of great choices besides college—at least give yourselves the benefit of starting strong, you know?"

Bettina nodded. "We get it, Ray. Promise."

"Good, 'cause I'm ready to get to the fun stuff." Ray engaged the file and the show started. Applause and laughter livened the room.

Barker was just topping off his coffee when Elias Joss entered the small meeting room. The old friends met in the center and greeted each other with hearty handshakes and hugs.

"Look at you, all relaxed!" Eli raved, devilry and teasing vivid in his blue-green eyes. "Where was that relaxation in the tropics?"

Barker rolled his eyes. "Don't start, E."

"Hey, I'm just remarking on verified info." Eli spread his hands and backed away. "We all saw how you made a point of escorting Ray home."

"Just being a gentleman." Barker studied his coffee.

"Mmm..." Eli sounded far less convinced, while helping himself to juice from the beverage cart. "That why you weren't home all weekend? Being a gentleman?"

"I—wait." Barker turned. "How do you know I wasn't home all weekend?"

Eli grinned. "I didn't, but thanks for the confirmation."

Barker made a gruff sound. "Dumbass," he muttered.

Eli chuckled over his juice. "So? What gives, man?"

"It's confirmed. They want me for the programming board."

"And you accepted."

"No. And I won't. They're up to something."

"They?"

"Harold and Cole."

"What are you thinking?"

"That they're being strong-armed. I need to find out by who. I have a feeling the reason has to do with all that property being bought at five times its worth."

"Well, aside from the initial sales, there's been nothing," Eli shared. "No bids for construction or renovation. Zip."

"I need to get in there—inside that building," Barker spoke as if to himself.

"No, B, save that for Sophie and her people." Eli referred to Chief of Detectives Sophia Hail Rodriguez, who was married to one of Eli and Barker's best friends, Santigo Rodriguez.

"Don't worry, I won't do anything stupid," Barker said with a smirk. "I'd appreciate you not saying anything to Sophie. I don't need much attention on this yet."

"And why do you think there's anything going on? Could be there's nothing that warrants the next WPXI exposé, you know?" Eli shook his head, reading the look Barker sent his way and knowing his words would do nothing to sway the man's hunches. If Barker Grant thought something was up, chances were strong that there was.

"Did you stop by to toss ideas at me about your next move?" Eli asked.

"Actually, I came to talk about our next trip."

The topic shift threw Eli for a moment. Mouth open, glass poised for sipping, he gaped at Barker.

"What's up?" Barker gestured with his glass. "Think we could interest the group in another trip before Christmas?"

"What the hell for?"

Barker shrugged and sipped more of his coffee.

"Jeez, Bar, she really got to you, didn't she?" Eli raised a hand when Barker stepped up to argue. "And don't tell me this isn't about you making things clear to Ray regarding how you feel about her. Guess you didn't get around to discussing that this weekend."

"Please don't give me a hard time about this, and whatever you do, don't say anything to Line and Tig."

"You're joking, right?" Eli let out more laughter for good measure. "Do you think they didn't see all the same things I did? It's been obvious for close to a year that you've got a thing for her." Eli settled back on the edge of his desk to fix Barker with a concerned glare.

"Must be pretty intense if you're still trying to keep quiet about it—needing to leave town again to tell her. Where are we headed, by the way?"

Barker didn't appear eager to share. "Switzerland."

"Switz—"

"Klosters," Barker added before Eli could finish his incredulous reaction.

Eli whistled. "One of your family's places. So...you want to *leave* snow for more snow."

"Technically, we haven't had a *real* snow yet," Barker argued. "But yes, I want more snow—keeps people closer to home."

"I get it." Enlightenment dawned in Eli's eyes. "Smart."

Barker headed back to the cart for more coffee.

"So what's really goin' on here, man?" Eli let his concern filter in more intensely. "Why so driven with this? I mean, Ray's a peach, but I get the feeling something else is up with you."

Barker stopped his movements at the cart. "Would you think I'm an idiot if I told you I think she's it?"

A slow grin curved Eli's mouth. "Since I already think you're an idiot, the answer would be no. I get how you feel." He seemed to sober. "I get it because the same thing happened to me when I met Clarissa. She...she came out of nowhere—hit me like nothing I could describe. No, B, I won't think you're an idiot, but why all the theatrics? Just stay home and tell her how you feel. Clearly, you can hold a conversation with the woman. You've been chatting platonically for almost a year, you know?"

"I know that." Barker set aside his mug, deciding against more coffee. "I just think her head's someplace else."

Eli waited, able to tell that the details were difficult for his friend to share.

"She's not taking my calls," Barker eventually confided. "I called her the night after I left her place—I didn't think much of it when she didn't get back to me at first. I figured she was preparing for the work week and all. But—" he knocked a fist against the cart "—it's been almost a week now and…"

"Maybe she's trying to tell you friendship's all she has time for."

"I don't think that's it." Barker walked around the office, his gaze fixed on the downtown view beyond. "I think she's counting on me *not* calling so she can give me a way out."

"So you'd rather her be more direct about telling you to stay out of her life?"

"Funny. She doesn't want that. I know she doesn't."

A new realization took hold of Eli's expression then. "You're really in love with her, aren't you?"

"I barely know her."

"You've known her almost a year."

"I just don't want her to go anywhere."

"Except Switzerland."

Barker winced, looking to Elias. "I'm gonna need your help with that."

"Need me to talk Miss Moni into letting you have the place, huh?" Eli laughed, referring to Barker's mother, Monika Grant. "No problem, I'm her favorite, anyway."

"I thought that was Rook."

Eli took no offense at the sly reminder. "Well, seeing as he's on his honeymoon…"

Barker grinned. "Don't worry. I don't need you to talk to her."

"Ah, jeez." Eli cringed. "Please tell me I don't need to talk your Uncle Dale into it."

"Forget it, no one could talk that man into anything

unless it was to ask if he could be an even bigger jack-ass than he already is." Barker sighed. "I actually need you to talk to Ray—encourage her to come along. Tell her you're celebrating the anniversary of your first date with Clarissa or something."

"That's pretty weak, B. Why can't you just—"

"She's not taking my calls, remember? Besides…she already knows I've got money. Seeing a place like the one in Klosters, she'd probably be even more against getting involved with me. Money and the fact that I've got a ton of it won't do me any favors in winning her over."

"And yet the Klosters is where you want her."

"The Klosters is where I want her," Barker confirmed.

"I won't bother reminding you, you've already done that—won her over. Ray's a pretty straight shooter, B. I don't think she'd have invited you to her place, and definitely not for the entire weekend, if that hadn't happened already."

"I still want to play it this way, all right? Just act like the place is part of some deal you found."

Eli inclined his head, considering.

"With the weather changing, you guys won't be quite so busy." Barker referred to Joss Construction, which Eli ran in partnership with their longtime friends Linus Brooks and Santigo Rodriguez.

"Guess I could do that. Might work well with what I'm planning anyway."

"Which is?"

"Not yet." Eli's gaze took on something distant yet hopeful. Soon, he was fixing Barker with a challenging look. "The question now is, will you do what you need to once you get there?"

"Now that I think about it, I guess most of the hard conversations I've had to have with Sophie were only hard because we waited so long to get them out in the open. Don't let this fester, Ray."

Ray looked at the mug of tea she'd been nursing since shortly after her arrival at the office of Philadelphia DA and Ray's newest friend, Paula Starker.

"That's easier said than done," Ray mused.

"Hmph, don't I know it?" Paula returned. "But it has to be done, especially in situations like this. It's not just about you and Clarissa. You guys have employees for the club and potential students for the hoped-for studio to consider."

Ray left the cozy living area where she and Paula had talked for the last twenty minutes. "I don't want this to be ugly, Paula."

"Do you think it could be?"

"No." Ray waved off the possibility. "Clari isn't unreasonable. She loves the girls and really does want what's best for them. She just thinks the way she's going about it is the only way to honor Miss Jaz's wishes."

"Just remember, you've known Clarissa for a very long time. I'd say that puts you in a position to know better than anyone how to get her to see what's best for everyone involved."

Ray turned from observing the small, dazzling Christmas tree in Paula's office. "You sound just like Barker," she said.

Paula's brows lifted, the comparison stirring her intrigue. "Did he tell you that in the Bahamas?"

Reading the underlying question, Ray turned back to the tree. "Stop, Paula."

"What? I know what good…friends you are."

"Don't even try it." Ray downed the last of her ginger tea that accompanied lightly iced cake squares and fruit. "I already talked to Clari. I know you're all *curious* about Barker seeing me home."

"I swear we thought nothing of it." Paula's lips twitched before she giggled into her mug.

Ray shook her head. "It's a good thing you're on the right side of the law. You can't lie worth a damn." Inwardly, Ray mused over how funny life worked out sometimes. While studying the elegance of the stately office, she would have never believed *she* of all people would be friends with anyone in a position of authority, let alone a bona fide district attorney.

Paula Starker, however, was no ordinary DA. She'd grown up similar to Rayelle—underprivileged, but determined to make it. Their choices had been vastly different, but Ray supposed in the end, they'd both triumphed over their ghosts. They'd achieved success in their own ways, but triumph was triumph.

"I'm sorry." Paula was recovering from her giggle fit. "We all think it's pretty great—you and Barker. We just don't get why you're beating around the bush this way."

"Mmm…says the woman not sure if she's coming or going when Linus Brooks is the topic of discussion."

Paula smiled in spite of herself. "A side effect of having history. You and Barker don't have that kind of trouble. You've got a clean slate."

"You know who his family is, don't you?"

"I know who *he* is," Paula countered. "*He's* all you should be concerned about."

"All right." Ray studied the downtown view and warmed at the sight of the holiday season claiming the decor of the buildings and lampposts lining the streets.

"Let's talk about who he is," she said. "Respected, award-winning, intelligent—one of the last remaining very eligible bachelors, considering you, Sophie, Viva and Clari have taken the others off the market, and he's supposed to pick me?"

"*Supposed?* I'd say he's already made his choice. I'd say you have, too." Paula let the observation rest for a while and then clapped.

"I'd also say you could use a good party. You should come to my annual holiday mixer. I host it at my place out in Chestnut Hill. You can even spend the night— I've got plenty of room."

"Who else is coming?"

"Barker is on the guest list."

Ray winced. "I haven't been taking his calls."

"Do you want him to stop calling?"

"No." There was no hesitation in Ray's response. "I just don't want to get my hopes up. It only makes it harder—"

"If he proves he only wanted to enjoy you in bed for a while and that's it?"

Ray flinched as if the words were a blow. "Can't get the possibility out of my head."

"You know—" Paula stood then "—the only way to know for sure is to put yourself out there and see."

"That part I know." Ray gave a self-conscious smile.

"Just not so sure I want to know the rest. The illusion is a lot nicer to take."

Paula shrugged. "So enjoy it then."

"Right…" Ray gave a little laugh. "That's just the kind of woman I don't want him to think I am."

"What kind of woman? One who knows what she wants and goes after it?"

"Come on Paula, you know that's not always the best course of action for women who come from pasts that are against them."

"And if I'd let my past keep me powerless to go after what I wanted, I'd have nothing."

"But that's about *things*, not—" Ray stopped then, understanding her friend's point.

"Yeah." Paula nodded and smiled. "I let my past dictate how I should handle things with Linus, too. I wouldn't want you to go through that kind of torment, Ray. I don't think I'd have my worst enemy go through that kind of torment."

One of the phones began to ring on Paula's desk. She raised a finger and headed over to the long, mahogany-brown furnishing. "Let me take this, and we'll pick things up after."

With Paula gone, Ray fixed on the view. Tucking into her chair, she wrapped herself in thought and considered her friend's words.

# Chapter 6

A smile livened Ray's face as she made her way up the walkway. After several days of playing catch-up with her schedule, she finally had time for a visit to Endeavor House. She wasn't expected for any volunteer duties that day, but there'd be nothing out of the ordinary about her just deciding to stop by. She often did that whenever her days at Jazzy B's were light.

Good fortune seemed to be on her side that day as she headed up the uneven concrete walkway and found Suzanne Jessup on her way down. She took the smile the young woman gave upon spotting her as a good sign.

"Your friends tell me you're a working girl these days," Ray called as she exchanged a hug with the young woman.

"It really *is* a good job, Ray. Busy, but good," Suzanne said.

"Leona and the others say you've been sleeping a lot on your downtime."

Suzanne gave a lopsided smile. "It only seems like it because I work close to third shift hours instead of the kind that keep me up with everybody else."

"To hear your friends talk, it's like a combo of second *and* third shift."

"Only seems like that, Ray…" Suzanne sang the words, but they held no trace of agitation. "I have to leave early because the buses don't run that far, but it's only an extra block walk. Security brings the waitresses home when they work third shifts. It'll be better once they get the place off the ground."

"They."

Suzanne shrugged. "'The Club' for now. No official name yet—we're still in the opening stage."

Ray studied a windblown pebble on the walkway. "What kind of club is it?"

Suzanne fixed her mentor with a measuring look. "I know what you're getting at, and it's not like that. It's more like a lounge, you know? People come there to drink, unwind, just chill."

"People."

"Men, Ray, all right? Men, women, everyone in between." Suzanne huffed. "It really is a nice place. It'll be even better once they get the remodeling done."

"But they're paying you like everything's fully operational?"

"Mmm-hmm, they're doing a lot of business." Suzanne's nod was an eager one. "I may be able to get Leo, Bet and Jani jobs when they really get underway. Let's see how much they complain about sleep when they're banking seven-hundred-dollar checks every week."

"Every week?" Ray's tone revealed her suspicions all too clearly.

Suzanne shook her head, followed up by a characteristically youthful roll of her eyes.

"Okay, look." Ray huffed then, squeezing her hands to stifle irritation. "I only want to know you're okay, that you're not being pressured into anything that'll make you uncomfortable. I guess alcohol's being served at this club."

"Here we go." Again, Suzanne performed her dramatic eye roll. "Ray, *please* don't mess this up."

Ray gave a dramatic shrug in return. "How can I do that when I don't even know the name of the place? Unless...you want to give me the address?"

Suzanne's expression screamed no. Instead, she leaned down to put a kiss to Ray's forehead. Suzanne Jessup towered over her leggy mentor by nearly a foot. "I love you for caring, Ray. It's a nice feeling when you've never had it."

Heart thoroughly melted then, Ray forced away her suspicions, as well as the cautionary voice telling her to worry. An after-hours dive with no "official" name and willing to hire underage workers to serve alcohol bore closer inspection by those with more authority.

"Get me a name and landline number as soon as you have one—"

Suzanne began to squeal her approval.

"Keep your phone on—Suze? Keep your phone on so I or someone here at the house can check on you when you're there." Ray took the girl's arm and squeezed.

"I'm gonna need you to take those calls and get back to us in a specified time frame. Understood?"

Suzanne was already nodding fiercely and smiling her agreement. "I promise, Ray. I promise." She tugged Ray into another hug and forehead kiss, and then looked toward the street.

"It's the bus." She broke into a light jog. "I need to get some stuff before tonight! Thanks, Ray!"

Ray returned the kiss Suzanne blew her way before disappearing into the bus. "You're welcome," she said, too low to be heard. She watched the bus roll away with her young friend in tow.

It wasn't her job to run down all the monsters, Ray told herself. In truth, the most she could hope for was to be able to tell her young charges what the monsters looked and sounded like before she sent them off into the world to do battle. It would have to be enough for now.

She tuned into the sensation of her mobile vibrating at her hip. Readying herself for Barker's name on the screen, she brushed her thumb across the protected glass and blinked when she saw who was calling.

"Eli?" she answered, smiling when the man's rich laughter seized the line.

"This a bad time?" he asked.

"No, no, I—I'm just surprised to—is Clari okay?"

Eli's laughter hit the line again. "I wouldn't be laughing if she wasn't."

Ray closed her eyes. "Right." She sighed.

"There is something, though. I…uh—you think you could stop by my office to talk about it? I'd meet you at Jazzy B's, but I can't risk Clarissa knowing about this yet."

Ray nodded. "All right, I understand. I'll be there soon."


"A little off the beaten path, huh, boss?" Sam Haynes said as he studied the area.

In response to his partner's uncertainty, Lucas Cumming's laughter echoed in the dim book- and paper-lined space. "I gotta agree with Sam on that one, Mr. G."

Barker took no offense and barely fixed the new reporters with a glance. "There's a good reason for it," he said. "I'm supposed to be backing off the story and leaving you to handle it. Wouldn't look too good for the newest member of the programming board to be seen breaking the rules, and fraternizing with underlings at that."

Sam and Lucas were still laughing as the rest of the investigative team trickled in.

"Let's get started, guys," Barker called as the audience found seats or leaning posts from which to listen in. "I'm gonna need a team to be my eyes and ears for a while. I'm taking a little more time off while I decide on this promotion."

"You deserve it, boss," Este Mintz called from her stance against a wall of magazines. "You can count on us to hold up our end."

"Thanks, Es, but you, all of you, should know this won't be that easy. Willard Harold and Garrett Cole want this story buried—my guess is it's nudging up against someone with the pull to get it silenced. Why, I don't know. What I do know is they'll weigh in pretty heavy on you all to do just that—bury it." Barker shifted his position on the stool he occupied in the center of the room. "That's actually not a bad idea, unless any of you have something to make it worth the headache it's been."

Este looked to the young man and woman standing nearest her in the dank workspace in the offsite storage building where they met. The duo exchanged looks of their own before turning to Barker.

"We did a little surveillance while you were in the Bahamas," Shaye Reed said.

"The area isn't as abandoned as we thought," Harvey Olssen added.

"We already knew that," Barker said. "The people who populate it are the reason I want you all to stay out of there."

"We never would've been on that end if we hadn't seen Steven Saltzman over there."

"Saltzman." Barker narrowed a look toward Harvey. "The head chef at LaMours?"

"Very same," Este confirmed. "Chesne Younce from the daytime squad's been hoping to get some quotes from him about the new management LaMours is rumored to be bringing in. Saltzman's been giving him the runaround, which of course has Chesne thinking some kind of scandal or worthy scoop is in the works."

"He caught a break seeing Saltzman heading out a back exit from LaMours around ten o'clock one night— and a Friday night at that," Harvey added.

"Strange for a head chef to be dipping out like that on the busiest night of the week, don't you think?" Este mused.

"We figured he couldn't have been going more than a few blocks away, but he went all the way to the west end, near some of the abandoned rail lines."

"Harv's right," Shaye confirmed. "A taxi driver would have to be tipped pretty heavily to drive out that far," he added.

"It's where our story is," Este said.

"Did Chesne ever talk to him?" Barker asked.

Harvey was already grimacing. "By the time he rolled up, Saltzman was already in his car. He said to hell with it and headed back to town."

"Guess you guys had a different experience when you went out to surveil." Barker observed his team curiously. "What made you ask Chesne about this?"

Shaye was the brave soul who spoke first. "Well, we all heard him griping about his wasted drive out to the boondocks. He kept talking about having Garrett and Cole reimburse his gas—called 'em cheapskates. His words, not ours," she hastily added.

"Point is, he was pretty specific about where he was going," Harvey said. "The questions were just begging to be asked, boss."

"Yeah," Barker agreed, albeit quietly.

"With the exception of a few locals—"

"And she means a *few*," Harvey interrupted Shaye. "The place was like a ghost town."

"But our destination was a whole other story. Lit up like Christmas out there, it was," Shaye added.

"The first two floors, anyway. Isn't that what you said?" Este queried.

"Right." Harvey sent the woman a sidelong smile.

"We could hear music, laughter—it sounded like a grand old time in there."

"And was it?"

"Can't say. We couldn't get in to make a visual confirmation. Sorry, boss." Shaye gave a sad smile. "Apparently, entry is only granted by invitation. We couldn't have talked our way in there if we'd tried—the place was locked up good and tight."

"We even tried to get the locals to tell us what was up," Lucas Cummings chimed in.

"You mean, what info you could intimidate the locals into divulging."

Lucas looked to Sam Haynes, who visibly tensed over their boss's reminder. "You heard about that, huh?" Lucas asked miserably.

"I heard about that," Barker said.

"We're sorry, boss." Sam sighed.

"Forcing people to talk is never the way we do things, regardless of what we suspect them of hiding." Barker issued the advice with a grim face.

Sam raised his hands defensively. "Got it, boss."

Lucas parroted the defensive pose while nodding.

"It does sound like there's a special list for admission," Harvey noted. "If the people we saw leaving there were an example."

"What do you mean?" Barker asked and listened as Shaye supplied a who's who list of visitors to the buildings on the "wrong side of the tracks."

"What are you thinkin', boss?" Este inquired.

Barker rubbed at his jaw for a long while before he spoke. "Not among the city's most squeaky clean, but definitely among the most prominent. I'd think the lesser knowns would mingle in that world to some extent. Chefs from upscale eateries or other service positions might rank an invite from upscale clients."

"But an invite for what?" Barker muttered a curse. "We may be flying blind here guys, until we find someone willing to talk."

Harvey and Este wore twin expressions of satisfaction. "We may have figured out that part, boss," Este said.

The offices of Joss Construction were as impressive as the structures they were often commissioned to build. As a woman with an eye for design and detail, Ray enjoyed taking time to observe craftsmanship that wreaked of care and talent.

Too bad that day wasn't slated to allow for such enjoyments. She'd been unable to think of little else aside from running into Barker once Eli called earlier that afternoon. Although he'd said it all had something to do with a surprise for Clarissa, Ray had already been the victim of her friend's well-meaning omissions. A chance meeting with Barker at Joss Construction could be wrapped up quite nicely into that vague chat she had with her best friend's boyfriend a short while ago.

She was shown to the executive wing with speedy efficiency upon her arrival. Ray hoped her smile didn't betray too much of her relief when she saw Eli stepping into his office. Alone.

"There she is!" Elias Joss's warm greeting was followed by a hug and forehead kiss before he stepped back. "Thanks for coming by to see me, Ray."

"It was no trouble. I had some unexpected free time. Plus, you have me curious."

"I'm going to ask Clarissa to marry me."

Mouth open, Ray didn't know whether to gasp or speak. She dropped into the nearest chair instead.

"I know it's early," Eli said.

"I—no, it—it's perfect. When?"

"That's actually why I called. Ray, I'll need a lot of help to pull this off if I plan to surprise her."

"What do you have in mind?"

"How would you feel about another trip?"

Eli laughed when Ray's expression screamed anything but approval. "That good, huh?"

"I'm just—it's a busy time, Eli, especially now…"

"I know, and I understand time is precious, but you know Clarissa would want her best friend there to put her stamp of approval on it."

"Yeah…but, Eli, I wouldn't know how to put together an engagement party to save my life."

"You don't have to. All you'll need to do is show up—will that work?"

"Well, sure, but I—that's not the point."

"Maybe this'll help. It's in Switzerland."

Again, Ray felt her mouth go slack, and slacker still as Eli relayed the travel details, including a chateau in Klosters.

"Extravagant," she breathed, impressed.

"We both know she's worth it." Eli strolled the room at a slower pace. "There's a problem with my plan, though. Fancy chateau or not, I can't take Clarissa there without knowing if it passes inspection. That's where you come in. I can't do it. She'll miss me if I take off so close to the holidays."

"And it's not like I've got anyone special to miss me."

"Ray—"

"It's all right, Eli." She was happy to feel her suspicions ease over the fact that the meeting wasn't part of some arranged get-together between her and Barker.

"I'm not trying to take her there until after Christmas. I want to propose on New Year's."

Ray nodded, pushing out of the chair she'd collapsed into. "This place you have in mind—is there some reason you don't trust the folks you're renting it from? I'd expect Klosters to have the most excellent accommodations and the personnel to maintain them."

"Too bad I don't know the personnel. Websites and blogs have nothing on actual time spent at the location."

"I can understand that."

"I booked it for a week before asking if you'd go. Feel free to think about it."

"I don't need to." Ray studied the view and then turned her back on it. "I don't guess Clarissa will mind since she was asking me to take more time before we left the Bahamas." Besides, she thought silently, it'd give her time to come up with just the right way to talk to her friend about their employees. In the end, their mission was the same—promoting and protecting the welfare and success of those young women.

"When do I leave?"

Eli collected the portfolio from his desk. "It's an open-ended ticket. You can go and return anytime between now and Christmas."

"What excuse do you suggest I use for Clari?"

"Yeah, I guess you're right…all that new business has got to be keeping you guys jumping."

Ray smiled in spite of the truth. Eli was right. Jazzy B's was no longer the premiere gentlemen's club of Philadelphia. It was now the city's premiere upscale nightclub. The establishment's nightly intake had proven that change in direction had been a profitable one. Yet another reason for her to get a move on with the discussion she'd been avoiding with her best friend.

"I can be ready to go by the first of next week," she said, telling the voice calling her a coward to shut up.

Eli rushed over to squeeze her arm. "Thanks, Ray."

"I'm looking forward to it," she said, meaning it. Anticipating her travels, Ray tried very hard not to think of what else the unexpected trip would help her avoid.

"You know there's only one thing I want for my birthday."

Barker smiled and settled in for a more comfortable position, and to enjoy the warmth of his mother's voice through the phone line. "Birthdays are about getting what *you* want, not about wishing things for other people. Sometimes it's okay to be selfish, you know? Why don't moms get that?"

"I can answer that in one word—kids." Monika Grant laughed over the line. "And for your information, this *is* what I want—to see you happy with something other than your job."

"You're sure it's that? Or maybe because all my cousins are either married or serious about somebody?" Barker laughed. "That's actually how it is most of the time, you know? Why harp on it now so much?"

"Because *now* two of your friends are married—one is in a serious relationship, and Lili says it won't be long before Eli proposes to Clarissa David." Monika referred to Elias's mother, Lilia Joss.

Barker reared back in the cushioned dark blue swivel and smiled while running his finger over the bridge of his nose. Moments later, he began to laugh again.

"I know you've got to be curious about what it must be like to wake up to one woman every day, Bari?"

"Well, it definitely sounds like *you've* been thinking about it," Barker teased, still laughing. "Is there something you want to tell me?"

"Oh, hush!" Monika Grant worked at seriousness, but she was soon laughing almost as heartily as her only child. "I just can't stop hoping that one day you'll bring someone you're truly serious about to my birthday party."

"I'll consider bringing someone serious, if you consider having a serious party—as in one."

"Hey! I can't help it if one of your grandparents' nights of debauchery was timed just right for me to be born so close to Christmas."

"You know, Ma." Barker winced. "I really didn't need a night of grandparent debauchery stuck in my head."

"Anyway, I can't help it that most of the family holiday gatherings turn into some sort of party for me."

"Sure you can't."

"I'll just enjoy having you bring a girl you're really over-the-moon for, making one of these stale parties less stale. It'd sure make the headache of having to deal with your father's family much more worth it."

Barker's laughter surged more robustly, before he sobered. "I'm working on it, Ma." His dark eyes were fixed on the front of the room that he alone occupied.

"I'm working on it," he repeated, and ended the call to enjoy watching Rayelle Keats enter her club.

# Chapter 7

"Getting chilly out there." Kennedy Wright laughed at the look she got from her boss.

"I'll say." Ray shrugged off a denim jacket that could've used a few added layers of lining against the increasingly frigid air.

"How 'bout a nice cup of tea?" Kennedy offered.

"Just what I was thinking." Ray closed her eyes as an image of a steamy mug of the lemon blend she kept in her office came to mind. "I'll grab some in my office."

"Oh, Ray, let me," the small, curvy blonde offered. "Besides, you've earned the chance to take off more time, especially when the place is like this."

"Closed?"

"Quiet and lovely," Kennedy said while punishing her boss with a sly nudge. Her powder-blue gaze went dreamy then and slid toward the main floor. "Mysterious," she continued, "sexy, built…"

Ray's frown arrived with a mix of confusion and amusement as she studied her lead bartender.

Kennedy caught the look, lifted a slender shoulder and then waved toward the dance-floor area. "You've got a visitor."

Ray didn't require visual confirmation to know who the unexpected visitor was. She took a look anyway, sighed and then wholeheartedly agreed with Kennedy's assessment.

"I'll go take care of that tea."

"Forget it, Ken. I'll need it more later."

Kennedy left her boss with a smile as Ray made her way into the space. It wasn't exactly dark, but dim and lit by fat, candle-shaped lamps that adorned the tables. Only a few had the lamps in use, including the one occupied by her visitor.

"Seeing as how you won't take my calls," Barker said by way of greeting, and stood. There was no accusation in his soft voice.

"You didn't leave a message." Ray's voice was equally soft. "I guessed it wasn't important."

"I didn't want to talk to your machine, but you."

"I suppose I was trying to make the point that you didn't have to."

"I know I don't *have* to Rayelle. I want to."

"You're a smart man, Barker. I think you know what I'm trying to say."

"I'm smart, not psychic Ray. Maybe you should just tell me what you're trying to say."

The easy expression she was trying to maintain tensed. "We had a fun night—"

"Weekend. A long one," he clarified. "I think I got there Friday morning, left sometime Monday." He inclined his head and wore a mock expression of confusion. "Is that right? I kind of lost track of time—so much to do and see…" His gaze traveled the length of her.

"Maybe we should leave it at that." Her tone was quiet. "No need for you to make more of it than it was."

"Do you want to make more of it?"

"I don't expect that."

"That's not what I asked," he challenged and knew from the belligerent flash of her gaze that she would never answer the question. She was too tough to admit such a thing. He'd wager she had experienced too much in the way of heartbreak by admitting such things. She didn't trust him enough. Lucky for him, the last was a thing he could change.

"How 'bout a tour?" he asked, and could see that he'd thrown her off guard. He shifted his smile and regarded her expectantly.

Ray glanced around the floor. "Doesn't look much different than when it was Jazzy B's," she said.

"I never came here when it was Jazzy B's." Barker spared another look around the space, as well. "Eli would've considered it a betrayal, I think."

Ray nodded, understanding and recalling the bad blood between Elias Joss and the woman his father had wanted to leave his mother for. Instead of making more of it, and more than ready to get out of answering his previous question, she gave a curt nod and turned.

"Well, we've expanded this floor—we've kept the stage." She headed toward the front of the expansive room. "It mostly serves as a second level to the dance floor, but we're starting to book more live acts, so hopefully that'll be a more permanent thing soon."

"How are the previous clientele handling the change?" Barker asked.

Ray smiled and considered her answer. "It's been tough for some of the regulars, but you can't hide quality, even when it's hidden beneath a racy but modest server's uniform." She moved them on through the club.

"Clients can now rent out the rooms that used to accommodate private dances. They can hold private parties, meetings with their choice of the servers who'll work them. Overall, the club's doing pretty well, but it's the private events that are putting us way over the top in revenue." Rayelle escorted Barker to the wing that housed those rooms.

"Speaking of parties," Barker said, "I heard you were at Paula's thing the other night."

"Oh? You...uh...you *heard* that?"

He grinned, taking note of his poor attempt at understating. "Her fiancé and I go back, you know?"

Ray had to laugh then. "So you heard that, too, I see?" She referred to the news that Paula Starker and Linus Brooks were engaged. The couple had made the announcement during Paula's annual Christmas party the night before.

"It was great seeing them so happy after all that," Ray mused while leading them through the network of corridors winding through the club. "Makes me think of the way things change—sometimes for the worse, but sometimes they do get better."

Barker whistled as they moved into the next phase of the tour. The club's loft lounge had remained virtually untouched and was decorated with widescreen TVs in every corner. Life-size framed portraits lined the walls and featured several servers in sexy, yet tastefully tailored outfits.

"This would be a good spot for an interview," he said while eyeing the decor with a complimentary gaze. "Wouldn't be hard at all to get a guy to spill most anything in here."

Ray couldn't resist laughing over the idea.

"What? I'm serious." Barker laughed and then resumed his appraisal of the area. "A man's brain would be close to numb taking in all the scenery. How are your employees adjusting to their new jobs?"

The question had Ray recalling what she'd confided to Barker about the effect the Jazzy B's changes had on the dancers.

"We've lost a few—not as many as I thought we would, but in a place like Jazzy B's, everybody's family…it's hard knowing that someone could walk out the door and you'd never see them again."

"Any word on what the ones who left are doing for work?" Barker closed his eyes and then gave a tight smile. "Just hit me if I'm asking too many questions."

"No, no, it's fine." Ray was on the verge of more laughter. To herself, she admitted how good it felt to be able to share her concerns.

"I've heard some of them left to do the same thing I offered them to do here." She gave a bewildered shrug.

"Couldn't buy into the changes?" Barker guessed.

"Well, in their *new* jobs, waitressing is just an added duty to dancing and...other things."

"I'm sorry, Ray."

"No need to be, but thanks."

"You talk to Clarissa yet?"

"Nah." Again Ray shrugged. "I'm gonna take more time to think about it."

"A lot of time?"

"Not much, but enough."

They'd made it to the office wing. A few of the waitresses were along the corridor and made no effort at hiding their interest or awe for the man they'd only seen through a screen or magazine page.

Ray held no grudges; moreover, she got a kick out of seeing Barker so humbled by his slew of admirers. The women cleared out soon enough, though, giving Ray time to resume the tour.

"Miss J's office is way too big for one person, so I've been sharing with Clari," she explained. "We're also using it as a meeting space. I think—hope, anyway— it gives the girls some comfort. We haven't changed much in here. We believe it comforts some of the girls— makes them feel closer to Miss Jaz, the ones who knew her. Well." Ray threw out her arms. "That about does it."

She was ready to lead the way back to the main floor and had reached the office door when it closed before her. Ray pressed her hand against it while Barker was drawing her back against him as it clicked shut. Like that, her legs had gone to water. "We can't." Her voice was a gasp, with his persuasive mouth at her ear.

"We already have," he reminded her.

"It won't work," she moaned, melting when he cupped and weighed her breasts while pampering her earlobe with a whisper-soft suckle.

"Bar—you, you have to listen to me—" She gave up, gave into his touch then. She was torn between pressing her point and focusing on the sweet, erotic rotations his thumb used to torment the peak of her breast, still confined inside her bra. She couldn't remember when he'd undone her blouse.

He stopped suddenly, and she moaned her disagreement with the move until she realized he had an ulterior motive. Barker had secured her back against the closed door. His gazed bored into hers as he challenged her.

"Why can't we, Rayelle? Because I'm privileged?"

She rolled her eyes, recalling one of several discussions that had occurred during the Bahamas trip.

"Did you think I'd take what you gave—what I wanted—and walk away like it never happened? You don't need to admit I'm right." He gave her space, but only a little. "We'll forget all about this, once you make it up to me."

Fire heated her eyes then. "Make it up?"

Barker maintained the innocent act. "Well, you don't just expect me to forget the way you misjudged me?"

"Misjudged—"

"I want to know you, Ray. In bed and out of it. You not taking my calls has already wasted a lot of time. The sooner you make this up to me, the sooner we can get on with getting to know each other."

Torn between exasperation and amusement, Ray took great pains to calm herself before she spoke. "How exactly am I supposed to make this up to you?"

"We'll talk about it tonight when I pick you up." His smile was devilment personified. As he'd suspected, her mouth fell open, and he capitalized by thrusting his tongue deep for the kiss he took while lifting her into him. Her legs were around his waist. The snug position inside the V-shape of her thighs merely heightened his need for more of her—all of her.

Ray had already submitted to the effects of the kiss, desperation alive in every slow stroke she treated his mouth to. Need had her so restrained in its clutches that she was pretty much unaware of the fact that she was trying to free herself from the shirt Barker already had half undone.

He ended the kiss with a scrape of his perfect teeth down the long line of her neck, only to hear the erotic hitches of her breath while she succumbed to her arousal. Only when Barker set her back against the door, stilling her hands by squeezing them inside his, did Ray snap to. She blinked rapidly, as though she were waking from a dream.

"Be waiting for me in your lobby at six," he said. "Don't make me come up there for you, Ray." He kissed her forehead, pulled her from the door and left.

Ray thought she'd latched on to a reasonable excuse for weaseling out of Barker's invite when she realized he hadn't told her how she should dress for the evening. Barker took care of that when he called her an hour after he left the club. She didn't hesitate to answer. It felt foolish to continue avoiding his calls, anyway. Besides, it wasn't as if she really wanted to evade them. Barker informed her that it was a holiday party and that most anything she wore would be fine.

With that settled, Ray accepted her fate and then criticized herself for acting like she had no real interest in going out with him. All she wanted was to be with him, despite the fact that she had a past that was working against her—one that was chock full of disappointments. She didn't want any of her time with Barker Grant to be one of them, and yet that possibility was virtually all she could think of.

"I was hoping you'd make me come up and get you."

Ray dashed the unwanted possibilities from her mind and turned to face Barker with a genuine smile already curving her mouth. "I love holiday parties and didn't want to risk missing one."

"That wouldn't have happened anyway. We'd have just been fashionably late—*later*," he rephrased with a slight shake of his head. "The party actually started at six." A broad smile brightened his face as he threw out a wave to security guard Oliver Dever before he relieved Ray of the wrap coat she'd been about to slip on over her dress.

Barker indulged in a few moments to size Ray up in the frock—a strapless black number with an intricately laced back and softly hooped ankle-length skirt. "Told you whatever you picked would be fine," he said.

"Is that a compliment?" She tried to tease in an effort to dismiss the heat working its way up her spine.

"Compliment? Damn straight."

The heat grew stifling. "Barker." She risked a look past his eclipsing frame to Oliver behind the guard's desk. It was far too late, however, to ward off the erotic heat radiating along her legs that attempted to ignite the familiar throb no man had ever been so adept at sparking. The ease with which Barker Grant was capable of doing so was close to frightening. "Stop," she murmured.

"I haven't done anything yet," he volleyed back.

"It's the 'yet' I'm afraid of."

He made a faint tsking sound. "There's that word again."

"We've got a party to get to, Barker." She reached for her coat.

He easily held it out of her grasp before reluctantly settling it over her shoulders and angled the dark wool so that she could put her arms in the sleeves. "Guess there's no point in asking where the party is or who's giving it?"

"You can always ask."

Ray shook her head. "Why do I get the feeling *I'm* the reporter tonight?"

"Role-play, Ms. Keats? I like it." He nudged her shoulder. "How 'bout we follow up with that later?"

Ray could only laugh as they made their way out the door.

"All right, where are we going and who's giving this party?" Ray's tone as she repeated the question clearly relayed that she expected a detailed response.

They'd taken the exit for the area of Mount Airy. The spot was undeniably impressive, and as well-known for its architecture as it was for its historic roots.

"Barker?" Ray had to resort to punching the thigh nearest her when he didn't look away from the road while navigating the Jeep along a ridiculously winding stretch of gravel.

"Cut it out," he hissed. "This road's no joke."

"You seem to be handling it well enough. So how well do you know our hosts?"

"Quite well." He smiled. "For as long as I can remember, actually."

Ray took note of the homes they passed. Some peeked out intriguingly behind majestic towering rows of trees fringing the outskirts of the properties. The homes, beneath the starlit sky and blanket of snowfall the area had seen earlier that day, was a breathtaking sight.

"Barker...come on." Ray's voice was close to a whine then as she wiggled against her seat. "At least tell me if I'm about to meet the mayor or the new football quarterback."

Barker's long, infectious laughter filled the Jeep's interior. "I can promise I'm not taking you to meet the mayor or the new quarterback."

Ray settled back in a new position against the Jeep's heated suede seats. She couldn't put a finger on exactly why Barker's words failed to instill the sense of calm she was striving for. Before she could circle around to a new line of questioning, he was pulling the vehicle to a halt.

Ray saw they were parked at the top of the horseshoe drive before a gloriously lit home of white brick and black columns. Against the snow, it looked like some sort of castle from a fantasy novel. She gave herself a mental kick and then called it all nonsense.

Perhaps, but it was no less accurate. Strings of golden

light encircled the columns while vibrant hunter-green garlands had somehow been decoratively draped over the white brick. The place was unbelievable.

Ray turned to share her opinion with Barker and found that he had already left the cozy confines of their ride. She watched him head over to greet the parking attendants with handshakes and shoulder claps like they were old friends. She saw him grin, and dear God, he was a gorgeous thing.

*Enjoy it, Ray. Enjoy it*, she chanted to drive out the pessimistic waves that hinted of problematic waters. The holidays were upon them, and she had the attention of a disturbingly beautiful guy, good sex, parties hosted by—the thought gave her pause—people he'd known for as long as he could remember.

"Who lives here, Barker?" she asked when he came around to open her door.

He was still grinning and completely unshaken. "I told you, they're people I've known a long time."

"How long? Since birth?" Ray felt her heart sink, rise and sink again when she saw the confirmation surge in Barker's dark eyes.

His hold on her hands tightened, and then he was tugging her from the car seat. "How 'bout we let this guy do his job, huh?"

Dazed, Ray saw one of the valets settling in behind the Jeep's wheel. She let Barker finish helping her from the seat. He was grimacing and then patting the pockets of her coat. Coming up empty, he felt his own pockets and withdrew gloves.

"Do you trust me, Rayelle?" He posed the question

matter-of-factly, while putting her hands inside the fur-lined leather gloves that were clearly too large for her.

"Yes," she answered in the same manner.

Barker smiled. Progress, he thought. Trust was a good start—the *best* start, actually. The rest would come later. Soon.

Finishing with the gloves, he squeezed her hands before tugging her in more closely.

Ray took comfort in the outline of his lethal frame against her. Disturbingly gorgeous, and sex appeal for days. *Head out of your panties, Ray.* She reminded herself that she was about to meet people he'd known for years.

She smiled, flexing her fingers in the oversize gloves. "We're about to go inside. My fingers would've survived."

"Listen to me, Ray." He gave her the swiftest of tugs. "You'll be on my arm in there the whole night. My family can be—" He paused at her gasp over the confirmation that she was to meet his family. "You're on my arm the whole night, remember?"

"What if I have to go to the bathroom?"

"I'll wait outside the door, unless you want me in there with you."

"Pervert."

"I prefer imaginative."

"You would." Her attempt at playing didn't last as long as she would have liked. "Barker...there might be people here tonight...maybe even some of your *own* family...who might remember me from Miss J's. She knew a lot of people who lived in places like this—*she* lived in a place like this. People who live this way—"

she seemed to shudder as though the idea were incomprehensible, despite the fact that she stood in the middle of it "—a lot of them patronize the same places, and Miss J's places drew a lot of powerful—"

"Ray. Ray? Stop." He bent a little to look at her more directly. "If this was all for my benefit, I don't need the warning. I don't want it."

"So you're saying you don't care?"

"I won't lie and say I'm not curious—it's in my nature to be. But that's beside the point. You're mine."

Ray had little time to fixate on her heart pole-vaulting to her throat before Barker was pulling one of her gloved hands over the crook of his arm and guiding her toward the wide porch before them. The steps were long, rectangular slabs of white brick that led to a set of wide double doors of dark pine. The doors were open to permit the interior's golden lighting to spill past the double glass doors to maintain the indoor warmth against the chilly night.

Ray curled her fingers into Barker's arm as her light eyes scanned the majesty before her. The porch columns looked as though they belonged at the entrance of some grand museum.

The guests still filing inside, attired in evening wear that whispered affluence and status. In spite of her nervous state, she took comfort in the spicy inviting fragrances that scented the air with festive provocation. The foyer seemed alive with the sparkling white lights that encircled additional columns that were smaller than their counterparts, but no less majestic. The vivid illumination was nothing against what waited beyond the foyer's towering archway.

Ray shivered, newly comforted by the pleasantly

warm air brushing her skin. Her coat had been removed by one of the indoor attendants, staunchly formal in a white tuxedo with tails.

"Okay?" Barker asked, smoothing his hands over Ray's shoulders beneath her gown's chiffon jacket.

Her nod was a dazed one as she took in the elaborate surroundings. She gasped when her eyes set on the massive tree tucked in the far corner of the main room they faced. Barker was shaking hands with the man who stood greeting the influx of guests. Ray pulled her eyes from the tree when she heard the man laugh and say Barker's name. She smiled, enjoying the happiness brightening Barker's ebony stare as he returned the warm greeting.

"Ray." He turned, drawing her closer. "This is Jack Lindsey. He manages this place."

Ray blinked, offering her hand and hoping she didn't look as surprised as she felt to be meeting a household manager. She didn't even think Jaz Beaumont had claimed one of those.

Jack's greeting was warm and genuine nevertheless. Within seconds, he had someone supplying her and Barker with flutes of crisp champagne. He then urged them to have a wonderful time, and Barker and Rayelle headed into the guest-filled main room

"Do you want to dance or eat first?" Barker asked.

"Why don't we just get the hard part out of the way?" Ray gave a sigh, as though to prepare herself. "You brought me here to meet your family, didn't you?"

"I certainly hope so!" an elegant female voice responded before Barker could reply.

The couple turned. Ray watched Barker lean down to

kiss the woman's mouth before setting his face against her neck. He straightened and turned to Ray.

"Rayelle Keats, this is Monika Grant, my mother."

# Chapter 8

Ray doubted there had ever been a time when she'd been so equally suspended between surprise and disbelief. Both, however, had stemmed from the fact that the dark, beautiful woman Barker kissed could have a full-grown son.

"No way," Ray heard herself breathe.

The unintended, audible comment summoned a hearty melodious laugh from Monika Grant. "I like her already, Bari!" she told her son.

"So do I." Barker's expression was fixed, and read of desire and approval.

"Well, yes, young lady, I'm in fact this guy's mother."

Ray closed her eyes briefly and swallowed. "Mrs. Grant I—I'm—"

"Don't you dare apologize. A comment like *that* is

*exactly* the kind of thing a woman wants to hear—especially when she's celebrating another birthday." Monika Grant's eyes sparkled with playful mischief and apparent satisfaction as she studied the woman on her son's arm.

"You've brought me a lovely one, Bari," she said. "I hope this won't be my only time meeting her."

"It won't be." Barker's tone was soft, and yet confirmation rang heavily through the words.

"Well—" Monika Grant gave Ray's arm a tug "—just in case it is, we should get to know each other. Go get me a drink, Bari," she said without a look to her only child.

Barker maintained his hold on Ray. "How about we all go?"

Monika rolled her eyes. "Ever notice how stubborn reporters can be, Rayelle?"

Ray laughed. "I have!"

"So how long have you and Bari been seeing each other?"

"We've been friends almost a year."

"Friends."

"*Just* friends, Ma." Barker knew all too well how… romantically his mother's mind could work.

"Interesting," Monika murmured. "How *very* interesting."

"You have a lovely home, Mrs. Grant." Ray observed her surroundings with renewed awe.

Monika Grant's expression was several shades removed from awe-filled. "It's my brother-in-law's place. My birthday's near Christmas, so it tends to be all about me this time of year."

"Like it wouldn't be, anyway." Barker used his free hand to draw his mother closer.

"Hush," Monika Grant ordered, even as she smiled over the kiss Barker put to the top of her head. "You need to be thinking about when you're going to bring Rayelle to see me."

"You know, you could at least give me the chance to ask her to come with me to your *actual* birthday party."

"Ah." Monika swatted away the plan. "I expect some time to get to know Miss Rayelle before that."

"Time to get to know what?"

"That's between me and Rayelle for now, isn't it?"

"I disagree."

Again, Monika rolled her eyes toward Ray. "Remember what I said about reporters?" She sighed. "Well, can I at least introduce her to the family?"

"Depends." Barker smiled when his mother laughed.

"Don't worry." She gave another wave. "*This one* only gets introduced to the best." With that, Monika took Ray's arm and led her on ahead of Barker and deeper into the gaily decorated room.

"Deb!" Moments later, Monika was calling out to a tall, willowy dark woman whose hair was pulled back into a severe bun that took nothing away from the warmth in her luminous maple gaze.

"Rayelle Keats, Barker's cousin, Debra Grant. This is her father's lovely house," Monika continued.

Debra greeted the new arrivals with holiday wishes and laughed as Barker drew her into a warm hug.

"Deb, Rayelle is Bari's friend."

"Ma," Barker called in warning.

"They've been friends for almost a year," Monika went on.

"A year?" The info apparently intrigued Debra, as well. She seemed to stop herself before tumbling too deeply into her aunt's speculation. "Well, now...that's wonderful."

Ray shook her head at the women. "You two make it sound like Barker has no friends."

"No lady friends," Debra clarified.

"None he ever brings to visit the likes of us anyway," Monika added.

"Hey!"

"Friends, Bari." Monika quelled Barker's attempt at disagreeing.

Debra joined in. "For almost a year."

"Mmm-hmm." Monika flashed an adoring look to her niece. "Friends, Bari, not flavors of the month."

By then, Ray was laughing over the serve and volley between aunt and niece and Barker's inability to do anything to stop it. She was still laughing when he took her arm.

"We're going to dance," he decided.

Ray only smiled as Monika's and Debra's laughter followed them.


"So... I'm a friend and not a flavor of the month, huh?" Ray queried when they were on the dance floor moments later. "At least that tells me your family doesn't know about our weekend together."

"That weekend meant a lot to me." His voice was as quiet as the look in his dark eyes as he gazed down at her from their embrace.

Ray was still smiling slyly until she noted the utter seriousness on his face. "It meant a lot to me, too." Her tone had gone equally quiet.

Barker cupped her chin on his palm before she could say more. Self-conscious then, Ray cast cautious looks around the dance floor, but saw that she and Barker didn't appear to be drawing very much attention from the room.

The trees, twenty feet if they were an inch, stood on either side of the dance floor. They illuminated the room with generous splashes of white gold. A trio of massive chandeliers poured similar lighting upon the dense crowd. The dance floor was decoratively sprinkled with a powdery dust that gave its users the sensation of twirling amidst snow.

"It's all just so beautiful," she breathed, wholly immersed in her surroundings.

"Ray?"

She didn't take note of Barker calling her name. "Gosh, that band—I heard them play years ago at a party I went to with Ms. J. Talk about an upscale crowd—"

"Rayelle?"

She heard him then, saw how serious he'd become. "Are you all right?" she asked.

"I'll be better when you start taking me seriously." He sighed. "Guess I'll need to tap into that fear of yours again before that happens, huh?"

"Barker..."

"I want what you seem hell-bent on withholding, Ms. Keats. I want you, and not only what you let me have in bed—your body—but all you have to give. I want it for a long time, Ray."

He didn't dare say he wanted forever—not yet. He wasn't trying to send her into a state of shock, but he needed her to know he was serious. It was clear she didn't think he was, if her smile was a hint.

"I think *you're* just feeling a little left out." Ray gave a flirty tug to Barker's jacket lapel. "All your friends are either married or about to be—"

"Ray—"

"Now, now, don't get testy." She savored the lightness of the moment as they danced. "Maybe you're feeling like you have to make the same moves, to get as close to meaningful as you can get."

Barker shook his head, silently marveling over how tough she was. So damned determined not to put herself in any position where she could risk getting hurt.

"Ray, what I feel for you has nothing to do with my friends." He grunted a laugh. "If it did, I'd have been in a serious relationship a long time ago. Tig, Linus and Rook have been in love with the same women forever, you know?"

"Mmm, and now Eli's about to join the club."

Barker spread his hands and then let them fall back to her waist, where they'd rested. "You've got me there," he said.

"See?"

"Mmm-hmm." He followed the admission with a kiss.

Even if she were a lovesick romantic, Ray believed she wouldn't have been able to conjure a more perfect moment. The music was sublime in all its mushy, holiday wonderment. It combined with the quiet lighting and the air that was fragrant with cider, cinnamon and all the appropriate aromas of the season, which sent her contentment into overdrive.

Correction, being kissed in such exquisite surroundings by the likes of Barker Grant sent her contentment into overdrive. He kissed her like they were the only two in the room. She heard the warning bells, but was too selfish about her pleasure to relinquish a moment of it. She could feel Barker's fingers slipping inside the heart-shaped cut along her dress's bodice, and intentionally heaved her chest to absorb as much of the caress as she could. She wanted him closer than what kneading his arms would allow, and was moving to encircle his neck when they were jostled by a passing guest.

"Easy, Bar, I'm sure the lady wouldn't mind being taken to a room."

Ray sensed the shift in Barker's mood with admirable speed. Quickly, she curled her fingers into his jacket sleeves to prevent him from going after the man who had commented. It all happened so suddenly, she was surprised she'd even thought to grab Barker as fast as she had.

"I'm all right," he said.

"Sure about that?" Ray kept her tone encouraging. "Because I'm seeing your face right now, and I think you're barely holding yourself back." She shifted to look past him. "Who was that guy?"

If possible, Barker's expression went chillier. "My cousin Dean—my uncle Dale's son."

"Debra's brother?" Her surprise was sharp.

"Yeah." Barker grinned. "Believe me, she got all the decency genes in the family."

"Guess I won't be meeting the rest of her immediate family."

"Not if I have anything to say about it. Introducing you to the slime of my relations isn't the way I'll convince you to become part of my family."

Ray reared back as though she'd been struck. She was sure she'd heard right, though unsure if she should remark on it. The decision was taken from her hands when someone called to Barker.

"Saltz!" Renewed surprise and quiet suspicion flavored Barker's greeting to the tall, stout man who had approached. "LaMours not keeping you busy enough? You're working the stoves here, too?"

Steve Saltzman laughed with all the gregariousness one would expect from a man his size. "I'm actually here as a guest."

"Well, well," Barker mused and then gave Ray a squeeze. "Rayelle Keats, meet one of the best chefs in Philly. Steve Saltzman."

*"One of?"* Saltzman faked offense while reaching for Ray's hand. "A pleasure, Ms. Keats."

"Same here. I'll have to put LaMours on my list," she said.

"Bring this guy." Saltzman inclined his head toward Barker. "Have him handle the check."

"I like that idea." Ray gave a savory smile and nudged Barker's side. "I'm gonna find the ladies' room. It was nice to meet you." She favored Steven Saltzman with a smile and moved on through the crowd.

"Barker, Barker, always finding the most incredible beauties to put on your arm," Saltzman commended.

# "FAST FIVE" READER SURVEY

Your participation entitles you to:
✱ **4 Thank-You Gifts Worth Over $20!**

## *Complete the survey in minutes.*

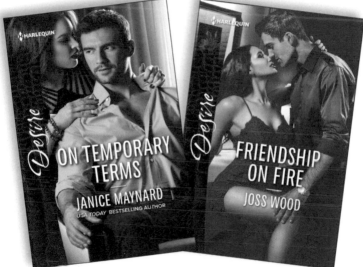

## Get **2 FREE** Books

*See inside for details.*

Dear Reader,

Since you are a lover of our books, your opinions are important to us... and so is your time.

That's why we made sure your **"FAST FIVE" READER SURVEY** can be completed in just a few minutes. Your answers to the five questions will help us remain at the forefront of women's fiction.

And, as a thank-you for participating, we'd like to send you **4 FREE THANK-YOU GIFTS!**

Enjoy your gifts with our appreciation,

*Pam Powers*

## To get your
## 4 FREE THANK-YOU GIFTS:

✱ Quickly complete the "Fast Five" Reader Survey
and return the insert.

# "FAST FIVE" READER SURVEY

| | | |
|---|---|---|
| **1** | Do you sometimes read a book a second or third time? | ○ Yes ○ No |
| **2** | Do you often choose reading over other forms of entertainment such as television? | ○ Yes ○ No |
| **3** | When you were a child, did someone regularly read aloud to you? | ○ Yes ○ No |
| **4** | Do you sometimes take a book with you when you travel outside the home? | ○ Yes ○ No |
| **5** | In addition to books, do you regularly read newspapers and magazines? | ○ Yes ○ No |

**YES!** I have completed the above Reader Survey. Please send me my 4 FREE GIFTS (gifts worth over $20 retail). I understand that I am under no obligation to buy anything, as explained on the back of this card.

## 225/326 HDL GM3T

FIRST NAME

LAST NAME

ADDRESS

APT.#

CITY

STATE/PROV.

ZIP/POSTAL CODE

HD-817-FF18

"Don't tell me you're here on your own? Or is this a scouting trip for your next gig?"

Saltzman chuckled. "I'm seriously here to socialize."

"Impressive—never thought I'd see the day. You live for the kitchen."

A hint of melancholy surged in Saltzman's blue eyes. "It's time I faced the fact that the kitchen won't ever get me a place like this." He scanned the grand ballroom surrounding them.

"So you're finally deciding to live." Barker nodded his approval.

Saltzman shrugged. "You could say that."

"I get it." Melancholy fused into Barker's reply, as well.

Saltzman appeared intrigued. "Reporter's grind getting to you, eh?"

"Just don't think I know what it's all for anymore—nothing changes." Barker sent a bland look around the room then. "Half the time I find myself asking if the things that *do* change are necessary. So long as no one's getting hurt or killed, why should I care about pulling the wool off and busting my hump to see they're brought to justice?"

"You sound like a man who needs to unwind, Bar."

"Workin' on it." Barker produced a purely devilish look.

"Right. Guess there's no need to convince you. I saw your lady. That serious?"

"What man wouldn't want it to be with a woman like her?" Barker spoke honestly, and not only to lure Steven Saltzman into a false sense of comradery so that the man would tell him what he wanted to know. He sighed, shrugging off the moment. "So, where's your date for the evening?"

It was Saltzman's turn to appear devilish. *"Dates,"* he clarified, and joined Barker in a burst of boisterous laughter. "Would you believe it if I told you I found something more satisfying than women?"

"Never."

"How about longer lasting?"

"Believable."

Saltzman rolled a meaty shoulder beneath his gray tux. "I may not have found a pot of gold in my kitchen, but that doesn't mean there isn't one to be found."

"Did you find it speaking in riddles?" Barker accused.

"Pays to be cautious, and anyway—" Saltzman gave a flippant wave "—such things wouldn't interest you, being heir to the Grant mega-millions."

Barker gave a wave of his own. "Sometimes a man needs to make his own way—with fewer strings. I like it that way."

"Hmph. I doubt I'd care about strings if mega-millions were involved."

"Walk a mile in my shoes, Saltz."

Saltzman looked to the Oxfords Barker wore. "Judging from the price tag on those, I'll take you up on that anytime."

There was more laughter, and the men parted ways soon after.

Ray appreciated finding the powder room free when she reached it after excusing herself from Barker and his chef friend. Powder *suite* was more like it, she thought, eyeing the space that radiated welcome and elegance with its white-oak-paneled walls, mauve throw rugs and upholstered chairs. Countless glass dishes carried individually wrapped hand soaps, lotions or other trinkets. Some fresh, fruity fragrance seemed to have been piped in through the vents, along with a quietly beckoning flute and piano piece.

Ray stood before the windows and absorbed it all. Hands folded beneath the scalloped edge of one of the cream-colored sinks, she forced her heart to slow its pace. The reaction had hit her out of nowhere mere moments before they left the dance floor.

The reaction may have been a surprise. The reason for it…well, she'd seen that coming all too well, hadn't she? Even so, she doubted she'd admit it to anyone— even Clarissa. She'd fallen in love with Barker Grant. Smiling then, Ray imagined Barker's shock were she to tell him that everything he said he wanted, she wanted, too. She probably had for far longer than *she* had even realized.

Still…she felt her hands unclench around the sink. She'd tried to talk him out of it. In spite of her feelings, in spite of his, Barker Grant deserved to be in love with a woman who wouldn't add a ton of baggage to his life. And, boy, did she have baggage…

Sure, she'd triumphed over much of it. She wouldn't be who she was without having done a great deal of that. Yet the sly comment thrown their way by his cousin had spoken volumes. It was just what Barker would be setting himself up for with her on his arm. Their relationship would be enough of a challenge. Left and right, they'd be fielding innuendos from outsiders who knew her late mentor. They'd assume her to be the woman's reincarnation. She wouldn't have Barker fielding such garbage from his own family. Regardless of whatever drama already existed between them, she wouldn't be the cause of any more.

It all sounded good in her head, but Ray knew it was nothing more than idle chatter on her part. She'd been out of her mind to let things go as far as they had. Likewise, she'd be out of her mind to end it.

With resolve fueling her smile, Ray approved of her reflection in the mirror. She gathered her things and left the powder room.

"Well, well, I'd heard Barker was here with a beauty, and I see that was no exaggeration."

Ray slowed her steps down the lonely corridor and turned to the man who had spoken behind her. There was no need for introductions. The man before her was an older but otherwise similar image of the one who had jostled her and Barker on the dance floor earlier. *Like father, like son,* she silently sneered.

"Dale Grant," the man said, "Barker's uncle."

She made no attempt at giving her name, but the elder Grant didn't miss a beat, moving the conversation along. Dale Grant's grin held more calculation than warmth. "I must say, my nephew never fails to make a statement—professionally or personally."

Ray turned to continue down the hall.

"He's outdone himself this time, though, bringing a girl like you around his family and their friends."

"You're about to fall through that thin ice you're skating on, Dale."

Ray tried not to appear too relieved at the sight of

Monika Grant heading toward them. She was pretty sure she'd failed at the task.

"Monika, this girl—"

"Shut it, Dale." Monika didn't stop until she had thoroughly invaded her brother-in-law's personal space. "You and your little boy should learn how to conduct yourselves around civilized people before you wind up leaving your own party in an ambulance."

"You've got some nerve speaking to me like this in my own home—"

"I'll have more than nerve, Dale. I'll have a hand putting you and my whiny nephew in that ambulance I just told you about."

Dale's lip curled and his lean frame seemed to swell with temper. "It's very cute of you to come to Miss Keats's aid, but I'm sure girls like her have a lot of experience taking care of themselves."

"Mmm... I agree, Dale." Monika gave a worthy sneer of her own. "Any girl can become an expert with handling pigs if she has the misfortune of running into enough of them."

Dale Grant stiffened, but he wasn't done. He favored his sister-in-law with a loathing stare. "I guess I shouldn't be surprised that you'd approve of Barker bringing a girl like this home."

Barker chose to head to the powder room and wait for Ray instead of spending more time inside the party. His mother would understand. Her actual birthday celebration would be upon them soon enough. Besides, he was damn well ready to grab Ray and get the hell out of there. It had been a mistake to bring her there.

While much of his family was a decent enough bunch, the few that made his teeth ache were enough to warrant skipping any occasion that called for them all to come together.

Barker took the turn leading to the guest washroom corridor at a relaxed stride that mirrored his mood just then. The party hadn't been a complete waste. Besides seeing his mother happy and dazzling that night, the talk with Steven Saltzman had been an enlightening one. The man had his entire hand in something that had him tap dancing on a cloud, and it was all taking place in the part of town Barker was investigating with little success. Barker's spot-on perception told him that Steven Saltzman could be the key to breaking that investigation wide open.

All of that could rest for now, Barker decided. A smile tugged his mouth when he saw Ray at the end of the long hall. The gesture died a slow death when he saw who joined her. His expression was unreadable for only a few moments before he saw his mother slap his uncle full across the face.

Ray gasped when she heard her name, hard and clipped, on Barker's voice. "I think he saw that," she said to Monika Grant.

"Get him out of here. Preferably *all* the way out," Monika ordered.

Ray was torn between wanting to catch up to Barker before his long strides closed in on them, and not wanting to leave Monika with her loathsome brother-in-law.

"Go!" Monika took the decision from the younger woman's hands.

Ray sprang into action, approaching Barker with a smile before he reached the other end of the hall.

"It's getting late and I'm all partied out—"

"What'd Dale say to you?"

Ray ignored the chill Barker's question sent down her back. "It's not important. Come on, let's—"

Barker squeezed Ray's hands gently and then set her aside.

"Barker, please." Ray stayed behind when she saw that Monika Grant was already on the way to offer her assistance. She noted that Dale Grant held his ground at the end of the hall.

"Bari." Monika pressed her hands flat and firm to her son's chest. "Look at me, baby." She waited until her instructions were followed. "Now, why don't you go take this lovely girl home and leave your idiot uncle to me?"

"Can't do that." Barker's voice was like stone.

"Would you feel better if I showed you two out?" Monika offered.

Barker's dark eyes remained fixed down the hall. "I'd feel better if I showed *him* out."

"And any other time, I'd enjoy seeing that." Monika patted his cheek. "But I'd rather you spend the rest of the night wooing this beauty, who I strongly suspect is about to be my daughter-in-law."

Thoughts of doing bodily harm to his uncle began to evaporate, and Barker smiled. "It's too easy for you to throw me off track."

"Don't blame me." Monika lifted her shoulders slowly and sent a look to Rayelle.

"Right." Barker smiled, offering his mother an arm. "Walk us out?"

Monika took the offered arm, squeezed it and sent a dismissive wave to Dale Grant, who stood seething at the end of the hall.

# Chapter 9

They'd been driving in silence for just over fifteen minutes when Ray spoke. The silence hadn't been strained in spite of the budding drama before they left the party. Ray supposed they were both just too exhausted for conversation. She hadn't exactly realized how wiped she was until she'd settled onto the heated suede seats of Barker's Jeep. The warmth was soothing, as was the added comfort of fine jazz that wafted through the state-of-the-art sound system. It all lulled her into a sense of complete and pampered serenity.

It had taken just over fifteen minutes to realize they'd missed the exit she had expected Barker to take to get her back home. Given the way the night had turned out, she wondered if he was simply taking a longer route to let off steam through the drive.

"Are we going to another party?" she asked when he took another exit altogether.

"Going to my place," he said.

Ray had no reply, not that she could've given one that'd be worth anything with her heart in her throat the way it was. With a mental jolt, she reminded herself unnecessarily that this wasn't the first trip she'd made back to a man's place following a party.

*Girls like me are used to such things*—the phrase had her cringing more for summoning it than over the fact that Barker's uncle had used it less than an hour earlier. She supposed that was the motivation behind the impromptu visit. Barker wanted to question her further about the run-in.

Before leaving the Grant mansion, Ray had overheard Monika Grant forbidding her son to follow up the night with any questions about what Dale Grant had said. Ray could tell by Barker's half-hearted agreement that he wasn't all that interested in honoring his part of the deal. She guessed they'd do well to go on and get the conversation started on the way to his place, but the plan was waylaid as they arrived at their destination.

Like the side of town where Dale Grant's deluxe spread was located, Ray had visited the Old City area Barker drove through now enough to know that it was another of the upscale locales. The spot was a huge draw for young professionals and those earning high six-figure salaries. The small borough just off the exit held a quaint old-world feel. Snow and festive twinkling lights cluttered in the corners of shop windows and around stately iron lampposts that spilled additional golden light to the ground. It added a heightened holiday air to the environment.

Barker stopped the Jeep beneath one of the towering posts, and like that, Ray's mind was back on the night's less-than-enjoyable moments. Barker left the car without a word and came around to open the passenger door.

"Can you make it up the steps in those, or should I carry you?" He sent a skeptical look toward the alluring heels she had selected for the evening.

The amused tinge to the question eased a layer of the tension Ray had been laboring under for much of the night.

"I can make it." Still, she took a steadying breath while eyeing the wide stone steps leading to the set of rust-colored doors behind tinted glass ones.

"Let's go then."

Together, they tackled the snowy path. Barker took Ray's arm near the porch while he unlocked the doors.

"Wow... I'll bet these two sets of doors come in handy," Ray teased.

Barker took it with good humor, his laughter easing yet another layer of Ray's tension.

"For all the good they do me," he said. "My neighbors prefer bypassing the TV and getting their news right from the source one of 'em, anyway."

"Your neighbors sound like smart people."

"In the summer it's just easier to leave the heavy doors open when I'm home." Following another wave, he directed her to precede him into the house.

The place suited him, Ray thought. There were tons of papers, books, journals and notebooks strewn across tables and stacked in corners on gleaming hardwoods.

The place could've easily been declared a warzone, but Ray could see there was a method to the madness. Spacious and stark, it managed to carry off a cozy warmth that was both inspiring and welcoming. It made Ray want to curl up in fuzzy socks with a mug of something hot and delicious and settle in with a story that would teleport her into another world.

Ray zoned back into the present to find Barker's unreadable stare fixed on her. He poured himself a drink from the small yet well-stocked and sturdy-looking cart across the living room. She spared another look around, scanning the crowded shelves lining the walls.

"Nice place," she said.

"Thanks. You can put your coat anywhere."

Glad for something to do, Ray removed her coat while Barker finished his drink. He went to take one of the lived-in armchairs that flanked the long sofa. Its fine tweed fabric gave an unpretentious quality to the room.

"Drink?" Barker offered when Ray turned from setting down her coat.

"I'm good."

With a shrug, Barker drained the contents of his glass in one long swallow and set the stout glass on an end table. The noise was more pronounced in the quiet. He offered his hand and Ray accepted without comment. She settled over him on the chair, her knees straddling his hips. The dress drew up to bunch at her waist, leaving her thighs bare but for the silken hose covering them.

Barker appreciated the barrier. There were things he wanted to say to her. He needed every bit of help he could summon to strengthen his willpower against her. The keyhole cut in the bodice, however, was a temptation all its own, and he had pitiful willpower against ignoring it, especially when it shelved her gorgeous breasts with such enticement. As though tugged by some unseen thread, his fingers found their way to the cut-out, where they fondled the supple honey-toned flesh. Her every breath sent the mounds heaving and enveloping his fingers when they dipped into the valley between.

Content, Barker rested his head back on his chair and delighted in the sensation of his fingers snug and warm where they rested. His thumb made lazy circles across her nipple and he smiled, feeling the bud firming in response.

Whisper-soft moans found their way up from Ray's throat. Her core clenched fiercely in response to the sensation that stirred when she moved against the wide, lengthy ridge of muscle straining his zipper. Ray threw back her head, clenching her teeth to stifle the moans he summoned from his stroking thumb.

"Ray?" He got no response, save her heightened moans, which were followed by a gasp.

"Ray?" That time, he squeezed her breast until she seemed to be tugged from her bliss. He smiled as her sex-drugged gaze slowly focused.

"What did my uncle say to you?"

Remnants of whatever erotic drug held her quickly dissipated. "Nothing important." Ray knew full well he wouldn't believe her if she said nothing.

Barker focused on his hand at her breast. The orb heaved with the same urgency as before, but he knew that urgency was fueled then by more unease than arousal.

"I'd like to know anyway." His bottomless eyes remained fixed where he held her.

Ray braced. "I'd like it if you didn't know."

"And you shouldn't be handling him on your own."

"Your mother was there—"

"She shouldn't be handling him either."

Ray gave a playful tug to his collar. "Thanks for going into protection mode for us, but your mom and I aren't so fragile that we can't handle an ass like your uncle Dale."

"I never said you couldn't—I said you shouldn't."

Before Ray could tease Barker about his reporter's sense for accuracy, she saw his expression turn even darker.

"He's done this before. Whatever he said to you tonight would only be the beginning. I'd like for that not to happen. It wouldn't be good for me to break an old man in half this close to Christmas."

Ray laughed. "So, you make a habit of bringing unacceptable girls home close to the holidays?"

Barker didn't find the remark funny. "I've never brought an unacceptable girl home—and neither did my dad, but that didn't stop my uncle from escalating from snide remarks to trying to force himself on my mother."

"Barker..." Ray shook her head. "How could you know that?"

Barker shrugged, continuing the sultry revolutions about her nipple. "My dad told me. The only reason my mom can hold me off is because I know my father already had the satisfaction of beating Dale half to death for it. I'm pretty sure my mother knows I wouldn't mind finishing the job."

"I'm sorry, Barker." She soothed his jaw with slow brushes beneath her palm.

"Just do what you can to stay away from him, okay?"

She smirked. "That shouldn't be hard. We don't exactly run in the same circles, you know? I can't imagine him frequenting the new Jazzy B's dance studio or nightclub." She was on the verge of laughter but saw Barker was still serious.

"As long as we're together, the chances of seeing my uncle are still pretty high, and I expect us to be together for a very long time."

Ray only swallowed visibly, trying and failing to speak.

Barker didn't appear to be waiting on a response. Again, he rested his head on the back of the chair. "Don't act like you don't know I feel that way—that it's been going that way for me. I've already told you as much. Hell, Ray, my mother can even see it. Won't be long before the rest of my family does, too."

Ray counted that as a fact. After all, hadn't Dale Grant alluded to as much just before his sister-in-law intervened? "I can handle your uncle, Barker. I've got a tough skin."

Barker didn't doubt that, even if the look and feel of her completely disputed it. His dark eyes followed the path his fingers took down her arm, covered by the sheer material of her dress's long, flaring sleeves. His gaze lifted when his fingers returned to her bodice and encircled the keyhole cut once again. Like before, he insinuated his fingers inside the heated dip between her breasts.

Barker used the spot for purchase and tugged on the bodice to encourage Ray to lean in until her mouth was fused to his. The kiss held an air of sweetness, but the moment was fleeting before the haze of full-on lust intervened. Their tongues tangled wildly, desperately and in search of supreme satisfaction. Barker's thrusts were pounding, possessive, his tongue taking her mouth with an eagerness that showed no sign of easing in intensity. He could hear himself moaning low in response to the slow, lazier thrusts she treated him to. The rhythm was hypnotic, virtually spellbinding, as were Ray's responsive breaths that carried a purring quality about them.

Her relaxed approach to their kiss merely heightened Barker's fierce manner. He abandoned her bodice where he squeezed and fondled both her breasts. His thumbs were working her nipples into pouting peaks that seemed to beg for the kisses he gave to her mouth. She felt his wide palms curving over her thighs, and she silently cursed that she'd had to don stockings for the evening.

"Mmm-hmm." She confirmed her approval when he gripped her bottom to draw her into a more snug fit across his lap.

Immediately, Ray resumed her sultry rotations, grinding with need across his arousal. Barker severed the kiss to drag his nose down the sleek line of her neck. All the while, he delighted in the confidence-boosting sounds she made. In moments, demand fueled his need and his grip on her bottom.

Ray realized he was milliseconds away from tear-

ing away the fabric of her hose, which was sturdy yet
could undoubtedly be ripped. She brought her hands
to his in a staying gesture and smiled. She savored the
power she held over the man who cursed his loss of
control, and she pressed his very appealing face into
the base of her throat while he seemed to be waiting for
his breathing to level.

Barker pulled Ray into a fierce embrace then. "No
going home tonight."

"Okay." She had no plans to argue and cherished
their embrace as it caused her shoulders to slump and
her eyelids to feel weighty.

"Ray? Ray." Barker knew the second call was un-
necessary. He could tell she was asleep by the slow
steadiness of her breathing. A quiet chuckle followed
closely behind his smile, despite the fact that he probably should have been a tad irritated that she'd just laid
waste to his plans for having his fill of her gorgeous
body that night. Instead of irritation, he felt a sense of
possession, followed swiftly by adoration.

During the span of the year in which he'd gotten to
know her, he had consistently fallen more deeply for
her. Sure, the initial attraction had been sexual. It was
insanity that any man could spend time with her and not
imagine what it'd be like to know she was his.

He stood then with Ray wrapped around him like
a child. Her long legs curled about his waist, her head
tucked in the crook of his neck as she dozed. She whim-
pered a bit as he took the first steps from the living
room.

"It's all right, sweet. We're goin' to bed." Barker

put a kiss to her head as she nuzzled it deeper into the side of his neck.

"Bed." She sighed.

Barker's chuckling resumed as he carried his provocative lady from the room.

He woke before she did and vowed he'd see that she got more rest while they were in Switzerland. It had to be exhausting running not one but two businesses. Especially two such different businesses. Between the budding dance studio and reimagined nightclub, she had to be doing more than burning the candle at both ends. By then, the candle had surely been extinguished.

Ray began to stir in her sleep and Barker knew she'd be waking before long. Until then, he satisfied himself with skimming his knuckles along her back and hip. He had awakened just before daybreak to check the mail and news—part of his morning ritual. When he returned to bed, Ray didn't awaken but wrapped herself around him like a vine. Barker wasn't the least bit driven to doze off—he was way more interested in holding her, watching her as she slumbered.

She stirred more when his fingertips grazed the curve of her breast, accessible where it crushed the side of his torso. Her lashes fluttered a bit more actively the closer she came to waking. Once she did, Barker tugged her hair and waited on her eyes to meet his.

"Was I sleeping?"

"Don't you remember?" He laughed. "You were out long enough."

Ray took stock of her position and saw that she was virtually nude but for the chiffon-fringed satin panties she wore. Barker had opted for more clothing, she observed. He was dressed in gray fleece sweats, slung low on his hips, hinting that he wore nothing underneath. Ray felt her body react with a reflexive throb. Sensing that he could feel her reaction, she began to retreat from her spot wedged against him.

"I should go."

Barker knew as much. Eli had kept him posted of her travel plans. She was heading out later that afternoon, embarking on the eight-and-a-half hour flight to Zurich, followed by an additional two hours via train.

Still, there was time and he was selfish enough to occupy as much of it as possible. He squeezed her hip before she managed to put too much space between them.

"You need to eat," he said.

"No time—"

"It only seems late." He steamrolled her objection. "It's not even eight thirty."

"I'm not hungry."

"That's surprising. We didn't eat much at the party— or after it."

There wasn't much Ray could say to counter that. She was certain that her stomach had started to growl fiercely before she'd even drifted off to sleep hours prior.

"You don't even have your clothes."

Naturally, that seemed to be the most viable argument. Gaze flaring, Ray sent a quick look around the bedroom, noting as she did that the space managed its share of relaxation amid starkness. She suspected that had much to do with the sparse yet compelling artwork adorning the walls and the single glowing lamp among several in the room.

There was no blinding sun streaming in yet. Chances were strong there wouldn't be, given the day was expected to be overcast and cold. Her eyes settled briefly on the worn, yet finely made chairs and sofa in search of her things. There was no sign of them.

"Would you have me leave naked?"

"I wouldn't have you leave at all, and definitely not before you've had your breakfast."

"And I need to be naked for that?"

"No." Barker pushed off the mass of pillows at his back and pounced. "You need to be naked for this."

He smothered any of her budding protests with a deep kiss. Ray's mind cleared of any such insanity, and she let herself melt back into the pampering mattress that had cradled her through the night. She gasped in the midst of it when Barker caressed her steadily tensing sex hidden beneath the middle of her panties.

Ray arched and opened herself to accommodate a more thorough caress. It was one Barker withheld until she punished his shoulder with a soft yet demanding blow. He needed only to slip his middle finger past the side stitching at the crotch of the satiny undergarment to ignite pleasure that seemed to shoot directly into her bloodstream.

The sensation plagued her with the most delightful vibrations. Greedily, her intimate muscles flexed and squeezed about the invading finger. When Barker broke their kiss to tend to her breasts, she bit her lip to quell the swirl of gasps and moans that flooded her throat.

What sounded like a sob did burst free, however,

when Barker lost whatever patience he'd been working with. He yanked aside her lingerie with such force, the material ripped clear up the middle. He offered no apology and only plied Ray's body with kisses that moved progressively lower, until his divinely gifted mouth was skimming her bare mound.

His nose treated her clit to a few lazy rotations before he sucked hard on the super sensitive nub. Ray shuddered even as she thrust herself eagerly against him. Barker left her wanting more, abandoning the still achy batch of nerves for the treasure beyond. He kept a hold on her thighs, keeping them spread so that she was secure in the position while his tongue plundered mercilessly and thoroughly.

"What about my breakfast?" she gasped.

A faint touch of Barker's laughter followed, and then his voice rose ragged and muffled. "Mine first," he said.

# Chapter 10

*Klosters, Switzerland*

Fall and winter had never been high on Ray's list of favorites. Though she'd grown up in Miami, where the time of year passed in a barely noticeable glimmer, the allure of it hadn't struck even after her move to Philadelphia. Ray knew it wasn't exactly the weather and the difficulties its harshness could render that fueled her indifference. More so, it was what the time of year signified.

Fall and winter meant the holidays. Holidays signified joy—the joy of family, to be more precise. Ray knew precious little about the joy of family. The colder times of year usually served as a harsh reminder of that fact.

As she looked out from her train window, with its

frosted edges, she thought that perhaps this place was just otherworldly enough to dispel those reminders. Klosters, with its frigid climate and stunning, snow-capped views, was a top destination for the world's elite. The spot catered to royalty and celebrity alike. Travel by train, cable car or bus was common. Klosters was home to just under five thousand residents, not including the influx of winter guests who craved its superb skiing environment and amenities. Much of its economy depended on the tourism industry. Ray could see that it was an industry worthy of the support it received.

The train stopped at Klosters Station, in Klosters-Serneus. At first, Ray was too enthralled by the visions of sheer brilliance before her eyes to tune into the fact that she had actually arrived at her destination.

"Mademoiselle?"

One of the station's attendants had called to her. Ray read his observation, noting that he seemed to be familiar with finding visitors new to the area all stricken by the same sense of wonderment. The slender attendant escorted Ray to the exit of the quiet, lavish car. His kind eyes and warm smile overshadowed the severity of his uniform and perfect mustache.

"Careful on the final step," he said. "The ice is even less forgiving than the snow, regardless of the footwear." He nodded approvingly to the stylish yet sensible pair of ski boots Ray sported.

Though another attendant waited to assist her from the bottom step, Ray took exceptional care. The last thing she wanted was to spend her time infirmed amid such beauty. The sun was high against a spectacular cerulean-blue sky. It kept its distance from the fat white

clouds also occupying the heavens and struck the un-
ending snow drifts with a blinding intensity.

The effect was so riveting that Ray squinted in spite
of the sunglasses she wore. The Alps were reverent—
gargantuan in the way they towered above the village.
It was a beckoning sight that she could have enjoyed
for hours.

Unfortunately, it was too damn cold to sit there and
be mesmerized. Blessedly, her ride to the chateau had
arrived. Her bags were quickly loaded, and she was ushered into the warm interior of a BMW SUV. She could
feel the warmth thawing her chilled bones within seconds of settling onto the seat.

Inside, she found a generously stocked mini bar complete with a tall, silver thermos of cocoa. She helped
herself to one cup of chocolate decadence and then another. She was halfway through her third cup when
she noticed they had traveled beyond the village. In
that area, she realized there was more distance between
the properties. The outlays were magnified in size and
luxury. The SUV took a sharp curve, and she could see
through the windshield what was to be her home for the
next several days.

Ray scooted to the edge of the seat, a gloved hand
tight around the passenger-side headrest. She gawked
at the approaching image. It was an eye-catching creation of snow-covered wood and multicolored stone.
Wide double doors were etched with a hand-carved
design—a Celtic symbol of sorts that lent a decidedly
old-world feel to the construction.

The non-conversational, but not unfriendly, driver
escorted Ray inside before he went back to fetch her

bags. Her accommodations may have shrieked old world from the outside, but the interior was a study in contemporary welcome. The polished hardwood flooring was decorated with generous rugs, thick and richly designed. A fire greeted her from a grand stone hearth. The flame glowed vividly in the sunken living room, despite the sun that still glowed superbly outdoors.

Ray found that the windows were high in that part of the house. She guessed it was necessary to hide the gleam she knew firsthand to be blinding off the snowy environment. Spotlights shone from beneath protruding panels along cream-toned walls. She tried and failed to hide a yawn. Already, the invitation to tuck into pampering coziness weighed on her heavily. A long L-shaped sofa with beige cushions and a smattering of tan and chocolate pillows appeared as a perfect oasis for a catnap. Admirably, she pushed aside the need, wanting to explore the amazing space for just a while longer.

The driver had returned and quickly deposited the bags in what looked to be a compact cargo elevator. "Your things will await you in your suite, Mademoiselle," he said. "For your first night with us, our premiere chef, Hilda Luzane, will arrive in a few hours with your welcome meal."

"Oh, that—that's wonderful, thank you." Ray was truly impressed and eager to enjoy the coming treat.

"It's a service we are happy to provide nightly and for breakfast, as well," the driver continued. "Mademoiselle need only call in her request."

Ray nodded. "I'll keep that in mind."

The driver gave a curt nod, yet his demeanor radiated welcome. "You will find phones in each room, all with direct lines to the caretaker's cottage—we passed it on the way in. Again, you need only call us with any questions or if there is anything else you require."

"I will, and thank you again." Ray offered the man another nod and grateful smile.

The driver graciously declined the tip she offered and made his way out. Once Ray was alone, she removed her coat and gloves while moving farther into the chateau. She smiled, observing the glasses waiting along with a bottle of red left open to breathe on the credenza just past the living room entryway.

Lamps were plentiful and washed the place in flurries of golden light. Delight multiplied when Ray wandered into the home theater that was furnished with deep oversize chairs that summoned sleep. Again, she pushed back those needs but knew her ability to resist had run dry when she arrived upstairs and found her bedroom suite.

The bed was a verifiable masterpiece that occupied its own alcove, with two sides fully devoted to windows overlooking the snowy cliffs and valleys. Drawn in, Ray took a seat at the head of the bed and surveyed the view. She thought of how much Clarissa would love it there. Elias had made a fine choice.

With a start, she reached into her back pocket for her phone. Eli answered on the second ring.

"Hey, everything okay?" His response was warm yet expectant.

"More than okay. This place is amazing." Ray turned to sigh over the view. "I only wanted to call before I got lost in luxury and forgot."

"Guess that means I made the right choice," Eli noted and then followed up with a laugh.

"It's perfect! If Clari doesn't accept your proposal, I'll personally take her in to have her head examined."

"Thanks again, Ray," Eli said, following more laughter. "So you're sure everything else is okay?"

Ray waved a hand. "Please, I'm fine—I've got everything I need, so stop worrying. They're even bringing me a specially prepared dinner in a few hours. I'm gonna look around this place a little more and then maybe take a nap. There are lots of really great places for one in this house."

"Sounds like you've got it all together then. I'll leave you to it."

"Oh! Eli? Um…have you talked to Clari? I mean, is she…uh…sincerely pissed at me for traipsing off on another vacation so soon?"

Eli chuckled a little before answering. "She's actually relieved you left."

"She is?"

Again, Eli chuckled over her evident disappointment. "She said she could tell you were still worn out from the Bahamas. She figures a few days away with no preplanned outings will do you well. A vacation doesn't feel like much of a vacation when there's an itinerary to keep."

"Amen." Ray sighed, looking back over the vivid skies and village from her vantage point on the bed. "It's really an unbelievable place, Eli."

"Thanks. Listen, you get some rest, all right?"

The connection ended, and Ray enjoyed the view for a while longer. She had every intention to get up and explore more of the house, but decided to stretch out first. She told herself she only wanted to take in more of the view, but sleep visited within minutes.

Night had fallen when Ray woke. She frowned, but not out of confusion as to her whereabouts. Instead, she lay there cozy in the decadent bed, trying to decide whether she really wanted to get up or just call it a night and burrow under the bed's thick linens.

In the end, it was her nose making the final decision. Her nostrils flared, having captured a whiff of something sensational in the air. Ray felt her jaw muscles react as well, clenching in response to the fragrance of beef and baking bread surging through the house.

She pushed herself up, glad she felt a lot more rested than she had before her nap. She hadn't bothered to change beforehand, but decided the least she could do was to get comfortable before diving into what was sure to be a dynamic meal. She had never had a meal prepared specially for her by her own personal chef, and she planned to enjoy the experience in comfort.

Ray moved on downstairs, attempting to be modest in a long, olive-colored flannel robe and matching fuzzy socks. The robe was only in case her cook was still on the premises. Otherwise, she was prepared to feast in the cut-off tee emblazoned with the word *Showstopper* stretched across her bosom. Rounding out the outfit were a pair of flannel shorts.

She yanked off the robe when a scan of the kitchen confirmed she was alone. Her doting chef not only left dinner, but also a large fruit basket with a card telling her to enjoy the meal and to call if she required anything more. Ray hugged herself while marveling over the slice of sheer perfection that had dropped into her lap. She abandoned the robe on one of the high suede stools along the bar that was fashioned behind the cooking island. She then focused on the kitchen itself. She hadn't expected the area to be outfitted in the same rich wood paneling as the rest of the house.

The effect was an eye-catcher, to be certain. Along with the wide cream-and-chocolate tiled flooring and black chrome appliances, the space was both functional and inviting. Soon, though, it was the appearance of another alcove that took the majority of Ray's attention. She observed the small table set for two, and a quiet approving smile tugged at her mouth. The kitchen was apparently on the same side of the chateau as her bedroom, for she was once again overlooking the mountainside. There was only a glimpse of the village below, however. The kitchen had a more direct view of the mountain range.

Ray's curiosity peaked and then dipped when she again observed the second place setting. Prepare for the unexpected, she supposed, and felt her stomach growl as if in response. She was moments away from turning to fill it, when the reason for the additional place setting revealed itself.

She smiled. A subtle, yet very appealing fragrance had lilted in along with the aroma of dinner. For Ray, there was no mistaking it. "Let me guess," she said. "Chef Hilda made all your favorite dishes."

"Not all," Barker said from where he stood behind Rayelle. "Some of my favorites can't be replicated."

Instead of moving closer, Barker leaned on the cook

island. "I didn't plan to surprise you too much. I was hoping for just a little touch of it, though."

"Oh, I'm surprised. Believe that." Ray steeled herself against telling him how good of a surprise it was when she faced him. He was an unarguable example of rugged sex appeal, she thought, taking time to regard him. The black bomber jacket was open over a gun-metal gray V-neck. The open collar of the black shirt beneath emphasized the powerful chords lining his neck.

"Do I pass inspection enough to stay?" he almost whispered.

Ray cleared her throat and tried to look nonchalant while Barker pushed to his full height. He eased his hands into the front pockets of the jeans he wore with hiking boots the same color as his sweater.

"What gave me away? Why aren't you as surprised to see me as I expected?"

"Something in Eli's voice," she said, grateful for the line of conversation. "He kept expecting something to be wrong or off-balance. At first I thought it was just concern over having me come all this way. Then there were the two place settings." She glanced toward the alcove. "And your cologne," she finished.

"Ouch." Barker made a pained yet adorable face.

Ray laughed. "It's a compliment. I only meant that I recognized it."

Barker studied the floor. "Does that mean I should keep it in stock?"

"Definitely." She felt him endear himself more to her with the dimpled smile he shared in return.

Barker masked his smile then as though he were a little self-conscious of his reaction. "The people who visit this place hardly ever visit alone—two place settings is standard."

"Oh, yeah?"

"This is an escape—a haven. A getaway for people to, um..." He wasn't quite sure how to continue.

"A place where people come to do things they can't do at home?"

"Thanks." Barker gave a quick thumbs-up. "But it's not the doing them at home part that's the trouble, but who they want to do them with."

"I see."

"Mmm-hmm, and have you also seen the bedrooms here?" His clear baritone had captured a softer chord.

Ray's gaze lifted toward the ceiling. "Only mine."

"Right." He nodded, remembering. "You were asleep when I got here." Once he'd made the discovery, he'd left her room knowing it wouldn't be long before he joined her if he stayed.

"Anyway, about the bedrooms," he went on. "A man with stockholders to please might not want them to know he likes to be tied down and ravaged by at least three women at a time."

"At least three." Ray lifted a brow, her expression obviously playful. "Impressive."

"Mmm," Barker confirmed. "Men in my family are known for their appetites."

"Your family?" Ray's playful expression began to sharpen.

Barker was beginning to look a bit miserable. "I own the place, Ray."

# Chapter 11

"Will you kick me out now?" he asked.

Ray didn't trust that she could speak, much less order him out. "Just...um..." she managed, "just give me a second to...to process that you own..."

"I don't exactly own it—it's a family holding."

"A family holding that could be yours one day?"

"That'll never happen." His appealing grin reappeared. "Cousins can be worse rivals than brothers and sisters." He was serious then. "So, will you kick me out? I'd understand if you did. My plan," he said, grimacing, and leaned on the island again, "it sounded less... deceitful in my head when I was coming up with it."

"Why'd you feel like you needed a plan?" Ray asked. "It's not like you needed to woo me into bed. I've already been there with you—several times, willingly and quickly." *Too quickly*, she added to herself.

"You regret it." Barker sounded as though he were reading her mind.

"I don't regret it."

"Liar."

"Why would I regret it?" When he only stared at her in reply, she laughed nervously. "Barker, we've known each other a year, remember?"

"And you still regret it."

"I don't regret it, I just…" She gave another look to the place setting. The glance carried more disdain then. "Do you know how many men have tried to…buy me in my lifetime? And this was a long time before I ever made my living on a stage."

"I know, babe." Barker couldn't help but clench a fist. It didn't take much to deduce that her foster-care upbringing had been far less than idyllic. "That's why I'm standing here now and feeling like scum. I never stopped to think what this would make you feel like. If it helps to know, I didn't bring you here because I thought you could be bought. I brought you here because I want more time with you—to show you I didn't only want you in bed and nowhere else."

"And now?" she prompted.

His dark gaze betrayed disdain then, too, as he looked around the kitchen. "*Now* it looks like I only want more time with you in bed, and *then* that'd be all."

"I know you didn't mean it that way," Ray said and watched relief waft into his expression. "What I mean is, I, um… I know when a man's trying to buy me— what it feels like to be nothing but a thing for him to wear on his arm or a toy for his bed. I know the difference between that behavior and when a man's trying to be nice." She frowned then, seeing coldness set into his fierce features. In a moment, he was leaving the island to block everything from her sight behind his impressive build.

"Nice, huh?" Barker gave a disappointed smile. "Wrong again, Ms. Keats. I sure as hell want you in my bed, and plan to have you in every one of them that's here before we're done. I've never had a toy like you there before, and I'd like to enjoy that a little longer." He spoke with matter-of-fact precision and no regret.

"As for you being on my arm," he continued, "I plan to keep on enjoying that, too. I'm no more evolved than the next guy, Rayelle. Maybe I'm worse. At least they were willing to let you go—to share you with the rest. I've never been good with sharing. I enjoy what I get and I keep what I want." He scanned the alcove before looking down at her again.

"I keep it in bed. I keep it out of bed. I brought you here to tell you that and with no distractions."

"Bar—"

"I'd like to convince you of that before we leave, but I'll take what I can get."

His intent was unmistakable when his fathomless stare roamed her scant attire. Ray felt the chill that had nothing to do with her bare legs and midriff. She managed a curiously amused smile then. "Do you mind if we eat first?" she asked.


"Once my dad and his brothers started getting married and having kids, it turned into something of a family place," Barker explained later as he and Ray took a winding back stairway toward the floor where she had been sleeping.

Dinner had been a filling experience, with a meal of tender sirloin tips smothered in a rich mushroom and red-wine sauce. The recipe was just the right accompaniment for the spinach-and-scallion-laced rice dish it had been heaped upon. Sourdough rolls marbled with pumpernickel accompanied the meal, which was rounded out by a comforting apple-and-peach cobbler.

"So, should I be offended that I was placed on the kids' floor?"

Barker laughed. "You should feel relieved. You'll see when we tour the other floors."

"Should I be nervous?"

"No reason for that—" he shrugged "—but people do tend to have an…um…a reaction when they see the suites up there."

"Now I think I'm more curious than nervous." Ray shrugged then, too. "Which way?"

Barker waved to indicate farther down the hall. Ray moved with confidence until she arrived at the short stairwell off to the right at the end of the corridor. She braced her hand against the wall, head bowed.

"Ray?" Concerned, Barker put a hand to her waist.

"This whole thing…you being here…*my* being here," she said. "Eli, he…um…he's really going to propose to Clari, isn't he? I mean, was—was that for real or just part of a set-up—"

"Honey, no…" Barker spoke in a soothing voice and shook his head with reverent regret. "No, babe, I swear it wasn't. Eli's probably been thinking of proposing to Clarissa since he met her. The idiot doesn't know if he's coming or going when she's around. When she's not around, she's in his head—and good luck getting him to make any sense then."

"Yeah." Ray had to laugh. "I think Clari suffers from those same side effects, too."

"I think I understand what they're going through." Barker's rich tone maintained its soothing quality. He inclined his head toward the stairway, smiling when Ray moved on.

The chandelier hanging dead-center in the wide hallway was the first thing that caught her eye when she stepped from the landing. The crystals reflected a mauve glow that cast a rosy tint to the white walls and sumptuous white carpeting that lined the space.

Barker's face held a subtle amusement that only made him more incredible to look at. "My dad and uncles never wanted to change it from the original design, so it's still got a sixties or seventies vibe to it."

Ray's quick laugh was flooded with curiosity. She kept walking, but matched her pace to Barker's as they ventured on. He took her elbow and squeezed to draw her focus to the door she was about to pass. He gave the powder-gray door a nudge open with a soft whoosh.

"Oh—" Ray had taken less than two steps inside when her sharp gasp mingled with more quick laughter. "Oh, boy…"

"Mmm-hmm." Barker leaned on the doorframe to watch and enjoy his guest's reaction. "The rooms on this level are actually called dens." He gave a slight shake of his head when Ray sent him a dubious look.

Ray's doubt soon shifted into a more dazed state the deeper she moved into the "den." The farther she trekked, the more fitting the name seemed. She found the walls adorned with oil paintings depicting coital-themed scenes against the backdrops of various periods in time.

She stared, mouth open, at the image of a pirate taking a woman against the wheel of his ship. Ray would've found the woman's attire more regal, were her luminous skirts not hoisted above her waist—not to mention her ripped bodice baring breasts crushed into the pirate's wide, sooty palms.

"Wow." She swallowed and turned from the painting, only to be newly stunned by the heart-shaped Jacuzzi tub upon an electric, candlelit platform. She wasn't sure what kept her in a greater state of awe—the tub or the immense bed set atop its own candlelit platform. It was equipped with an equally immense overhead mirror.

"Unbelievable...are all the rooms like this?"

"Pretty much." Barker loved the sight of her honey-toned skin darkening when she blushed. "The art gets a little more suggestive depending on which room you're in."

"I see, and are the whips and chains on the top floor?"

Barker grinned while levering himself off the door to head out. "Not quite." He scanned the area and smiled when she didn't follow. "It's fine if you want to choose a room here to sleep."

"I'll pass." Ray's tone was rather absent as she couldn't resist taking a moment to fantasize about her gorgeous host—his dark body sleek with cut muscles reflected in the gaudy overhead mirror. Eventually, she joined Barker at the door. In silence, they ascended another short flight of steps. The landing didn't carry them to another spectacular corridor, but directly into another room.

Ray wouldn't have dared to categorize the space as a den. This was an oasis for pure romance, more like a castle bedchamber with its stone columns and massive hearth waiting to glow from a fierce blaze.

Instead of the ostentatious white carpeting of the previous room, lovely yet understated woven rugs were strewn across the stone floors of this one. The room was dim and chilly, but seemed stamped with an undeniable warmth. This was a place where love was made, she decided. Once again, she was lost in the fantasy of her and Barker together before a fire in the cold hearth. Before she was wholly swept away by the erotic images, her eyes settled on the room's most breathtaking amenity. Her neck craning upward, Ray moved steadily forward until she stood almost directly beneath a skylight that was wider than the bed it sheltered. As the bed was a lake-sized creation, it seemed to set the skylight on an even grander scale. The construction appeared to take up more than half the ceiling and presented a flawless view of sky and mountains.

Barker had been moving closer to Ray for fear that her dazed movements while looking upward could result in her taking a bad fall on the stones. With that concern in mind, he went quickly to her, lightly guided her up the long steps and onto the bed's quilted burgundy comforter.

Still in her dazed state, Ray lay back and let herself be consumed by the unmatched beauty she witnessed. "Whoever built this had a fascinating mind," she said.

Barker was more intent on the woman atop the bed.

Idly, he toyed with Ray's hair, which was fanned out on the comforter. "The dome only *seems* fascinating. I guess the sky's the real draw," he said.

"Mmm…" Ray agreed and wiggled herself deeper into the bedding.

Barker had never been a big fan of the room. In that moment, however, he found it beyond beckoning. He knew that was because of the woman sharing the space with him.

"I bet your dad and uncles fought a lot about who got to use this room."

"Only a little." Barker turned his focus to the furnishings. "Once they started to marry, it went to the newest-wed couple of the group, and when that got old it just went to the folks who seemed the most in love."

Ray looked from the ceiling then. "I guess that'd be your parents," she said. "You mom seems like a great lady. I figure your dad must've been quite a man to land someone like her."

"He was." Barker's dark eyes filled with an unmistakable nostalgia. "Larger than life, my dad, but then he had to be to keep his little brothers in line." He shifted to a more comfortable position on the bed and smiled as he thought of his father. "My dad always envied what I had with Eli, Tig, Linus and Rook. He told me I got to choose my brothers. He said he'd always hated all the high-brow elitist crap the family liked to perpetrate. As I got older, so did I."

"So they didn't approve of your dad choosing your mom?"

"Not many of them—not at first." Barker grunted laughter. "And it wasn't because she didn't come from money. It was because she didn't come from money and still outclassed them in every way."

"Well, Mr. Barker Grant of the Delano Grants," Ray drawled, her mood light. "I'm afraid you've got the wrong girl if you think I could outclass anyone."

Barker clutched Ray's hand then, squeezing a little tighter than he'd intended. "I have exactly the right girl."

Ray rolled her eyes toward the skylight. "You mean the right one to aggravate your family?"

"I mean the one I'd like to add to it."

Ray's gaze flew from the skylight to Barker's face. "You've really lost your mind," she accused despite a suddenly slack jaw.

Barker squeezed her hand harder. "Then I'm sure you know it's best not to argue with a crazy person."

Ray doubted she would have argued with anyone— doubted her voice would or could do her the honor of showing up when she needed it to. His hold on her hand firmed again, and she scarcely registered it when he tugged her out of place to settle over him where he lay. Looking down into his striking face, she could detect the serious set to his features in the moon's vivid glow as it poured through the skylight. It was all she had time to consider before Barker took her mouth in one deep stroke.

Her reaction was instant, with triumph radiating throughout when she heard Barker's surprised and affected moan as he delighted in their kiss. The act intensified when his head lifted off the pillows to ensure his gifted tongue left no part of her mouth untested. He kept his grip on her hand as they kissed, while his free hand skimmed the length of her lithe body.

She was dressed in pitifully little next to him. As much as he wanted to come out of his travel clothes, he wasn't ready to release her yet. He continued his downward exploration until he was sliding beneath the waistband of her pajama shorts.

Ray was heatedly involved in the kiss but took time to delight in the soft squeezes he gave her bottom. She gasped in the midst of the kiss when he teased the intimate flesh there. She jerked suddenly against him when the teasing touch turned bolder and his finger entered her moistening core from behind.

Again, Ray gasped and arched to allow him more room to explore. Sensation pooled with fierce, unapologetic waves of pleasure. For a time, she could only rest her face against Barker's shoulder and absorb the waves thrumming her body. Selfish need plumbed her as completely as his fingers, and she gave into it.

She wasn't surprised that he seemed to sense when she was on the verge of peaking. He withdrew his fingers and took her mouth again before she could utter a word of protest. Faintly, she could detect traces of moisture on her skin and knew it was his fingers, damp with her need.

"Bar—" His name was muffled as their tongues tangled.

She barely registered when he put her on her back—never breaking the kiss or the liberties his hands took with the rest of her body. When he broke the kiss that time, it was to nibble his way from her earlobe to clavicle.

Barker's chest heaved as excitement and arousal had their way. Ray fought to keep her lashes steady and to keep her eyes open against the radiant skylight. The window was steadily becoming dusted with the snow that had intensified since they'd arrived in the loft room. The appearance of snow drifts amid moonlight left her almost as breathless as his touch across her skin. Barker's skilled, wondrously crafted mouth moved at a sleek, steady pace, closer to the energetic rise and fall of her bosom. For a moment, he debated against moving beneath the hem of her shirt or simply ripping it down the middle.

Ray arched sharply as his mouth cruised the swell of her breasts, while his thumb rubbed a nipple until it stiffened. She was desperate to have his mouth there. Ray crossed her arms at her waist and rid herself of the top. The material slipped from her weakened fingers when Barker cupped her breast for his mouth to take possession of the nipple he'd molested.

Her hands trembled as they cupped the back of his head. It wasn't long before his head ceased moving against her palms. Ray realized he'd continued his descent down her body. He plied the satiny dip of her navel with a merciless tonguing that tickled as severely as it aroused.

Instinct had Ray arching her bottom in anticipation of losing the flannel shorts she wore. Her breath hitched, enveloped in a sharp cry when Barker simply tongued her through the material, subjecting her clit to a fierce suckle that sent her fingers curving tightly into the bed's plush comforter.

Hearing her moan the first syllable of his name again, Barker made quick work of taking her out of her shorts, and then he was resuming his feast at her core. The influx of feeling saturated Ray's senses. She felt as overwhelmed by the remarkable beauty of the moonlit window as she was by the ravenous thrusts Barker used to take her to orgasm. When it hit, Ray didn't know whether to scream in delight or outrage. The influx of sensation magnified and then, like that, she was deprived.

He left her writhing in scorching need while he pushed up to jerk out of his clothes. Ray was unconscious of how her need ruled her as she shuddered and rolled on the mad tangle of covers. He removed his clothes with ruthless efficiency but took his time returning to the bed. He preferred to enjoy the sight of the honey-toned beauty he had there. She was a vision and desperate to have her arousal sated...by him. Ray gave an almost violent jerk in reaction to his touch when his hand circled the bend of her knee.

He shushed her, his mouth skimming the toned, silken line of her thigh. The directive silenced as his tongue claimed her sex once more. Ray could have arched right from the bed, were it not for his hand steadying her hip. She was secure there to accept his treat. Barker's moans mingled with hers when he felt her muscles flex around his tongue. Like before, he was attuned enough to her reactions to know when he'd driven her far enough.

Ray was dually pleasured by the captivating overhead view and the sensations occurring below her waist. She felt utterly adored and didn't think it got any better than what she presently endured. Then, Barker straightened, pulled her by her thighs to the edge of the bed and filled her in one lengthy, thick stroke. Her hips were high above the covers but, secured as she was, she couldn't arch or rock in approval. Barker had her positioned to his satisfaction and totally at the mercy of his desire.

Ray could only lie back and enjoy it. She wasn't about to complain. Barker took her with an intent deftness that stretched her fantastically. She threaded her fingers through her hair and absorbed every nuance of erotic bliss that zipped through her veins.

She could hear Barker's vocal reactions gain volume, and soon she was moaning over his release against the thin sheeting of the condom. It was like experiencing a massage within a caress within a massage.

Once Barker spent himself inside the condom, he kept Ray positioned for several moments after. When he withdrew, Ray had only a few additional moments to lie limp and sated on the well-used bed. Soon, he was returning and positioning her for their next round of lovemaking.

He received no complaints from her.

# Chapter 12

"As usual, your hunches are like gold, boss."

Barker grinned while dicing the last of the scallions on the chopping board. "She confirmed it?" he asked.

"Did she ever! A lot of bad blood still in the water from that marriage." Harvey Olssen's soft chuckle managed to plow through the line despite its low volume. "His habits really took them through the ringer, boss."

"Yeah...yeah, they did." Barker recalled the rumors of Steven Saltzman's gambling addiction. He'd known a different man when he'd first come to Philadelphia as a new chef eager to prove himself.

"He's a good guy in spite of that," Barker told his reporter. "I wouldn't like to see him go down that road again. So, um, no second thoughts about leaving him now that he's a big deal at LaMours?"

Again, Harvey chuckled through the line. "His ex—didn't sound like she had any second thoughts about calling a quits on the marriage. I asked and she laughed over the irony. Said working for LaMours only gave Saltzman a close-up view of the life he ruined their marriage to be part of."

Barker shook his head while setting the scallions into the fridge, along with the tomatoes, bell peppers and red onions he'd already prepped for the omelets he'd planned for breakfast that morning.

"Have you found anything that links him to my uncle?"

"Sorry boss, no." The apology echoed in Harvey voice. "Looks like being there was just more of the guy wanting a taste of the good life. What are you thinkin'?"

Barker wiped his hands on a dish towel. "I think it's time for Saltz to share the wealth."

Harvey's laughter resounded yet again. "Any plans for makin' that happen?"

"Workin' on it." Barker tossed aside the towel. "Listen, keep digging and call if you find anything interesting."

"Will do. Enjoy." Harvey urged before ending the connection.

"Yeah, workin' on it," Barker parroted his earlier reply, but was referring to a different situation entirely. He scanned his well-equipped cooking space. He'd started his prep work over an hour ago. It was creeping up on 9:00 a.m. but looked closer to 7:00 p.m. with the low-hanging clouds still lingering from the previous afternoon. Clearly, they were in for another blanket of snowfall. He was fine with that—it gave him a perfect reason to stay in for the day.

Ray had yet to emerge downstairs even after he'd put on a remarkably fragrant pot of coffee. He realized the aroma probably wouldn't reach her on the loft floor. And if it had, she probably hadn't awaken. He'd left her sleeping deeply and even got the monstrous hearth going with a fire before he headed downstairs. Between the fire, the dreary snowy morning and the decadent super king-size bed, he decided Ray had the right idea and heavily debated joining her.

Ray crept back into the conscious realm with a sigh. If anyone ever asked if she knew what real contentment felt like, she'd be able to tell them in strict detail.

Lying on her stomach, she treated herself to a languid spread-eagled stretch in the large bed. Slowly, she turned her face onto the other side of the pillow and cracked open an eye to search for Barker. She was especially surprised to find him gone. She could tell the room was a trace more illuminated than it'd been before she'd dozed off in his arms the night before. There was something else, though. The room seemed to carry additional illumination.

Taking her time—a lot of it—Ray rolled again, this time to her side. The covers were thick and pampering, so it took a bit of doing to shift easily beneath them. She caught an energetic flickering from the corner of her eye and gave a soft cry of delight. The blaze in the towering hearth was a glorious sight and almost as riveting as the skylight above.

She pushed herself into a partial sitting position and

smiled serenely toward the golden glow. The flame could have easily summoned her back to sleep. Apparently, Barker read her mind.

"Think I could get you to eat something before you conk out again?" he asked.

Ray scooted up, the feel of exquisite adoration still clinging as the linens bunched about her hips and left her bare from the waist up. "You don't know me as well as you think you do, Mr. Grant."

"I'll enjoy telling you why you're wrong, but do you think we could do it over breakfast?"

"One condition," she said. "Coffee must be involved."

"Well, well." His brow quirked. "There is. But you know, I once thought you were more of a tea girl."

Before answering, Ray spared a look around the enchanting room and the snow-sugared skylight. "Tea's great, but some mornings call for things with a little more kick."

"I'll agree with that more after you get something in your system." Barker made a terrific effort not to leave his post on the archway. Rayelle Keats was murder on his self-control.

Ray pushed to her knees. "That's kind of what I meant," she said.

"*I* meant food," he countered.

Ray responded with a theatrical sigh and a quick glance downward. "Should I go like this?"

"Check the edge of the bed," he instructed.

Ray saw the shirt he'd worn the day before. "I've got more appropriate things in my room, you know?"

"Doubtful. Put it on. Meet me in the kitchen."

\* \* \*

Barker had the coffee poured and bacon on to sizzle by the time Rayelle arrived downstairs. He nodded toward his shirt, which hovered just above her knees.

"Like I said, appropriate," he noted with a smirk.

Ray took a seat at the cooking island. She'd made a pit stop by her room for a pair of house flats. She had also considered dressing, but didn't want to be *too* inaccessible in case Barker had plans for them after breakfast. She was surprisingly comfortable given the vastness of the chateau. The place seemed quite easy to heat.

"The floors are even warm," she remarked.

Barker laughed. "You know black folks hate to be cold."

Ray enjoyed her seat on the high stool and appreciated being enveloped by the cushioned seating.

Barker watched his houseguest closer than he realized. He smiled while she leaned in to doctor her coffee with cream and sugar before gulping with intense desire. "It loses something when it's guzzled down," he cautioned.

"I disagree," she said.

Once half the brew had been downed, Ray sighed and smiled with renewed pleasure.

"Thank you." She squeezed the fat, glazed mug in both hands.

Barker offered a slow nod. He'd hoped she'd take the coffee at full strength. He was eager to see the exhaustion leave her lovely eyes.

"So, tell me about your volunteer work," he urged in

an attempt to keep her from questioning the concern in his eyes when he'd assumed she'd seen it.

Ray shifted to a new position on the generous stool cushion. "I'm working on some new ideas to encourage the girls to keep up with our visits. Things get harder the older they get."

Barker took sizzling bacon from the skillet. "You think they're losing interest in going along with the system?" he asked.

"Not really." Ray chewed her thumbnail and absently watched as Barker placed the strips on a napkin lining the platter. "I do think other things could compete for their time and influence them."

"Boys? Jobs?" he guessed.

Ray grinned. "Not much tops a paycheck—even a boy."

"Especially when you still live in that sublime period of your life when bills don't exist," Barker mused.

Ray laughed heartily. "Exactly!"

Barker pushed the platter of bacon toward Ray and smiled when she helped herself. "You're concerned," he noted.

She shook her head and crunched the bacon. "I know how seductive money can be with all its provocative ways."

"What?" He queried the change in her expression.

Ray only waved him off. "The independence that comes with making your own money—it's got a...way about it. Those ways can lead you to some pretty unfortunate decisions in the pursuit of holding on to it. Especially when it's the only consistent thing in your life. The one secure thing."

"Even the...*privileged* among us can understand that."

Ray smiled over Barker's outlook, appreciating the dig at his own background.

"Holding on to that one secure thing follows us through life, I guess." He shrugged as he added olive oil to a wide skillet. "The longer it does, the greater our chances for making unfortunate decisions that can be hard to reverse."

"Hard but not impossible," Ray said.

"True, but not all of us are blessed to see that—we just keep making bad decisions because we think we've gone too far to turn back."

Ray sipped her coffee, delighting in the taste. "Sounds like you've got some firsthand knowledge."

"Some." He pulled chopped veggies from the refrigerator. "I want us to have dinner one night when we're back home, all right?" he asked while taking more items from the fridge.

"I, um—" Caught off guard by the swerve in conversation, Ray stammered her reply. "If you want that."

"I want that." He studied her closely from the fridge and then gave a swift shake of his head. "It's for work," he said. "Someone who got caught up in the *ways* of money."

"Are we taking them to dinner to talk about it?"

"No. I want you to help me fulfill my cover-up with an...accessory on my arm." He sent her a wink and enjoyed the smile she returned.

"Sounds like fun." Ray sipped more of the coffee. "I get to see the mastermind reporter at work."

"Hmph, I don't know about the mastermind part."

Ray squinted her eyes in pretend concentration. "I

can think of at least three awards I saw at your place that prove otherwise."

Still, Barker looked unconvinced. "If I were a mastermind, I'd have figured out a way to get you to take me seriously a long time ago."

"Bar." Ray straightened on the stool. "I do take you seriously."

He stopped his prep work with the omelet mixture. "Seriously enough to be honest with me?"

"I have been." Her smile was genuine but quietly curious.

Barker's pitch stare was unwavering. "I wonder about that."

She stiffened. "Why?"

"Couple of things. We can start with you telling me what my uncle said to you."

"Provocative ways," she said after a few beats of quiet debate with herself. "He said women like me... our provocative ways cling to us like a film. He said most men could see that film, but others couldn't, and those were the idiots who convinced themselves that they were in love with such women, as if such women were capable of love. They were really only capable of lust and using it to advance themselves in life and status." She swallowed, more unnerved then by the sight of Barker's fist near the large knife he'd been using. "Barker—"

"What else?"

"Barker, I—"

"I know my uncle well enough to know the germ wouldn't have passed on a chance to run down my mother, too."

He gave her a crooked smile that she guessed was meant to be reassuring. If anything, it made him look more dangerous.

"We're in Switzerland, Ray," he reminded her with a sly eye roll. "It's not like I can just run out and beat him to death."

Ray didn't bother to point out that she knew him well enough by then to know he was patient. Patience could often yield deadly results.

"He, um—" She cleared her throat to buy some time, though that would solve nothing. "He said she had certainly used it to advance herself—that she'd even outlived his brother but gave him a fine son to ensure the bulk of the family fortune remained under her thumb."

Now, both Barker's hands were closed fists on the counter. His head was bowed, eyes closed, and Ray knew he was talking himself down and out of whatever lethal payback he was ready to inflict.

"That would've been the last straw," he said, almost in a whisper. "I might've killed him for that."

"Yeah." The word came on a sigh. "I figured as much," she said.

"You shouldn't have to tolerate that."

"I've tolerated that all my life." Her smile was content, resigned. "Sort of just rolls off after a while."

"Does it really?"

She shrugged over his doubt. "If I tell myself enough."

"I can't tolerate it, Ray."

"Well then, it's a lucky thing I don't have to spend time with your family. Besides, I met more people who were sweet than jerks. Your cousin Debra was very nice."

"Yeah, yeah, she is." Barker seemed to let go of some of the anger that was swelling his shoulders. "Guess we're lucky to have only a few lumps of crap in the family."

"So, will you stop worrying now?" Refreshed, she stood.

Barker grinned. "I guess I can—what? Ray?" He frowned, not liking the look on her face then at all. "Honey? You okay?"

"I am, I—" She tried and failed to complete the statement. She was the one bracing her fists to the counter then in an effort to steady herself. It was no match against the queasy feeling that had suddenly taken over her head and stomach. She gave an awkward look to her coffee then.

"Maybe I should be more of a tea girl." She tried to smile, but only managed a grimace.

Barker made no comment, though an element of knowing held his stare. When she put the back of her fist to her mouth, he folded his arms over his chest and seemed to be waiting on more to come.

Ray shoved from the counter, rushing toward a short hall, where a powder room was located. Barker gave her just over thirty seconds alone and then followed. He wasn't a bit surprised to find her heaving into the black porcelain toilet.

Ray was so wrought by sickness, she gave no reaction when Barker pulled back her hair to keep it as far from her mouth as possible. Her violent retching soon became a series of intermittent dry heaves. When they settled, she hugged the bowl as though she trusted it above all else.

Her grip was easily broken when Barker pulled

her close after taking care to wet a cloth and wipe her mouth. Ray turned her face into his neck, while Barker carried her back to bed.

She woke, finding herself once again in the midst of toasty warmth. She was back inside the loft bedroom and smothered beneath the many soothing layers of linens to protect her against the ever-present chill that the exuberant hearth flames hadn't been able to stave off. The skylight was an unintended conductor for the coldest air, as well as a masterpiece.

Slowly, she attempted to push herself up beneath the covers. She managed to prop on her elbows and look down at the pillow she was strongly considering putting her face back into. A short glass filled with a fuzzy amber liquid moved into view, followed by Barker's voice.

"Drink it."

He kept a strong grip on the glass even as Ray cradled it with a shaky hand and sipped. Ginger ale. She accepted the drink gratefully and was sitting up by the time it was done.

"Thanks." She wrapped herself loosely in the linens and tried to think.

"How long before you tell me I'm going to be a father?"

There was no need to speak once the question hit the air, but Ray tried anyway. Sputtering was all she could manage. The words *what* and *no* tried to make themselves known, but any truly cohesive sentence was a foolish hope.

Barker had no trouble speaking. "Were you going to tell me?"

"Barker, you—that's not—not." Ray shook her head violently until a wave of dizziness tried to creep in. "That's not possible…"

"How do you figure?" Amusement underscored his question. "I mean, I know your head's a little fuzzy but I don't mean this happened overnight. For some women the symptoms start right away—within a matter of days, in some cases."

She sent him a sour sideways look. "Thanks, Dr. Grant. I'm sure you remember all the condoms we used?"

"I remember. We used everything I had."

"See?" The question wasn't asked as confidently as she would have liked.

"You understand that condoms aren't one hundred percent effective, and we had lots of occasions to test those odds."

Ray felt her cheeks burn even as a chill kissed her skin. She knew it had nothing to do with the drafty space. "I wouldn't let that happen." She gave another belligerent head shake. "I'd never let myself get caught out there like that. I wouldn't do that to myself or you."

"Ray." Barker moved closer to the bed. "Do you believe I think you're trying to trap me?"

"Most men would." She winced. "I'm sorry. I'm sorry. I—I know you wouldn't, but saddling you with something like this wouldn't be fair—not to you and definitely not to an innocent kid."

Barker studied her closely and with a look of innate awareness. "You really don't know for sure, do you?"

"There's nothing to know." She made a push to leave

the bed but quickly reconsidered, not at all certain her legs would carry her.

"Do you always sleep as much as I've seen you do lately?"

"Barker!" she cried, feeling close to laughter of the hysterical variety. "We've been under the same roof all of a day—"

"Seen *and* heard—" he bulldozed her argument, "E says Clarissa hopes you'll use the trip to get caught up on your rest and stop sleeping all over the place."

Ray rolled her eyes. "Haven't any of you ever heard of jet lag?"

"Cute." Barker's glare said he really didn't think it was. "You're fortunate to have friends who consider all explanations."

"Well, this is one you *and* them can set aside." She raised her hands and let them fall to the covers soundlessly. "How could you possibly want to be saddled with something like this?"

"By 'this,' you mean our child?"

"Stop saying that."

"Hell, Ray, it's not the end of the world."

"Some women would think so." She scooted toward Barker's shirt, which lay crumpled a few inches away. "I won't take that back," she grumbled. "I know women who'd totally think that way."

Barker kept to his quadrant of the massive bed and idly studied the remnants of the ginger ale in the glass. "Do you think that way?"

"Doesn't matter." She jerked on the shirt. "It's not happening."

"Fair enough, but will you do something for me anyway?"

"Don't worry, I'll take a pregnancy test as soon as we're back."

"And you'd tell me? Whatever happens?"

At first, Ray felt a little miffed that he would ask such a thing. Yet considering what she'd just said, she couldn't blame him. "Of course, Barker. Of course I would."

He reached across the bed and pulled her close to put a kiss to her temple.

"I'll get a bath going in your room downstairs. It seems to help."

She laughed. "How is it you know so much about women and babies? Are you a closet ob-gyn or something?"

"Not at all." He took her hand, studying it while lacing his fingers through hers. "When I was about eight, I didn't like losing my best kickball partner. I needed to understand why."

"Kickball." Curiosity furrowed Ray's brow.

"My aunt Patricia. She could and still can play kickball better than anyone I've ever met. We used to play it almost every Saturday—her, me and my cousin Dale. Aunt Pat is his mother. She got pregnant with my cousin Debra, and soon her doctors were having her take it easy. They nixed our kickball games."

"Too bad." Ray sat riveted by the quiet nostalgia softening his features.

"Dale wasn't all that interested but I was, and so my education on the subject began. Anyway…" He got up from the bed, but stopped at the room door.

"Just to be clear, Ray. I'd want this. I'd want this all the way."

Ray didn't realize she was holding her breath until the room filled with the sound of a burning log splitting in the fireplace.

## Chapter 13

Ray decided that a hot soak in a deep, sumptuous tub was definitely *not* the way to get her to stop entertaining thoughts about napping all over the place. Yet she guessed since she was supposed to be pregnant, napping all over the place was expected.

Pregnant! She shivered amid the steamy fragrant bath Barker had been sweet enough to run for her. There was no way she could be…and yet…

Reluctantly, she recapped the state of her well-being over the last several weeks. It had only been a matter of weeks! The silent rant echoed inside her head. Ray sighed and kicked out at the foam topping the bathwater.

Weeks, even days, were all it took for such symptoms to show. She knew that well enough. Barker Grant wasn't the only one who had been schooled in the ways of what to expect when you were expecting. Hadn't her own mother made a habit of sharing—complaining about, rather—all her "delightful" moments during the nine months she'd been carrying her?

Barker hadn't complained though. He wanted this! He wanted her to have the child—if there was one. He *wanted* to be a father. She'd never known anyone who *wanted* such a responsibility. Nearly everyone she'd ever met or spoken to on the subject had viewed the possibility of having a kid as a chore they didn't want to be bothered with.

Ray thought of her mentor, Jazmina Beaumont. The woman had cared for Ray better than her own mother when she'd taken her under her wing at the tender age of eighteen. Jazmina Beaumont had come closest to being one who would welcome the responsibility of a child. Still… Ray felt her eyelids going weighty against the steam…perhaps Jaz Beaumont only felt that way because she didn't actually have a child. Despite her active social life, she'd made sure motherhood had never crossed her doorstep. Though she'd practically raised her niece, Clarissa didn't live with her. Clarissa had only spent the summers or the occasional holiday with her aunt, and then it was back to her dad in California.

No…no one she knew *wanted* the responsibility of a child in their lives. So why was the idea stirring a happy anticipation in the pit of her stomach, instead of the anxious, woeful one she'd expected?

Ray stubbornly refused to return to bed after the delicious bath. She could sleep at home. Her present digs were too incredible to be slept through. Besides, there were spots she was still a little curious about and wanted to further explore.

She found one of the heavy floor-length robes she'd packed waiting across the bed when she left the bath suite. She smiled. She'd purchased a few such items on a whim. There had been little chance she'd wear them during the recent trip to the tropics. There was even less of an opportunity around her own home, but here...

Ray smoothed a hand over the thick material. The robe hadn't been the only thing taken from her case. Barker had obviously unpacked for her. She guessed he intended for them to make the most of the trip, as well. She donned the garment, figuring it'd do well enough for house attire that day.

From the stunning window wall overlooking the surrounding mountains and village below, the day seemed to be enveloped by snow and clouds. It was a day made for staying indoors and exploring. She found her way to the kitchen, half-expecting to find Barker there awaiting her with orders for her to eat. The kitchen was empty, but he'd made his wishes known anyway.

She found a legal-sized sheet of copy paper and the word *EAT!* written in block letters in the middle and underlined for emphasis. At least he was giving her the chance to decide what to eat, she mused. Ray circled the island to the fridge, but didn't trust her stomach to hold a full meal. She selected a bowl of grapes and slice of cantaloupe instead.

Her appetite appeared and she gobbled down the fruit, chasing it with a tall bottle of water. Satisfied, she continued to test her legs by strolling the magnificent chateau. The walk was a pleasant one. Every corridor carried a beautiful painting, sculpture or amazing rug that brought an otherwise sterile space to life.

Ray wasn't at all ashamed to take the route back to the floor of the erotic suites. The rooms had secured a space in her memory that was sure to hold for a long time. They were a tempting sight with all the suggestive art and the mirrors above the beds. The corridor was almost as dim as it'd been the first time she'd taken it with Barker. The electric sconces cast muted, welcoming light across the space, which greatly ushered—instead of powerfully thrusting—one into the breathtakingly seductive chambers.

Ray peeked into several of the rooms. She wanted to indulge in a closer and lengthier inspection that she hadn't felt completely at ease doing before in Barker's presence. As she was on her own now, Ray planned to take a look at each of the spots before returning to her own room. She'd inspected three, when she noticed a mysterious flickering coming from a chamber farther down the hall. Only a second of hesitation, and then she was heading onward to ease her curiosity.

Ray was sure her gasp must've echoed down the hall when she pushed past the heavy open door. This was one of the rooms they'd skipped on the last tour. Since all the chambers were alike in their sensual design, she would've certainly remembered touring the one before her eyes then.

It was only similar to the others in size. The fireplace blazed with a fierce flame, which was what Ray guessed had accounted for the flickering she'd seen. Finding a fireplace of similar size to the one in the loft bedroom was indeed a shock, given the small size of this room. The hearth appeared even more gigantic, its flames even more dynamic. Somehow the room wasn't stifling, but comfortably toasty.

Alas, that wasn't what prompted her gasp. The other rooms boasted mirrors adorning the space directly above the bed. This room claimed an entirely mirrored ceiling.

One look at the artwork gave Ray a fine idea of what the space must have been used for. The mural covering the wall opposite the bed depicted an orgy circa early 1970s, given the afros and furnishings featured in the piece.

Ray didn't know whether to call the place tacky or inspiring. She wagered that it'd put the room's occupants in quite a mood.

"I didn't think you'd know what to make of this one, so I skipped it before."

She didn't turn at the sound of Barker's voice, nor did she flinch in surprise. She continued to stare in awe of the picture and the room's ceiling.

"They say the rich are different."

Barker grimaced, leaving the doorframe where he'd been watching her for almost ten minutes. "Not so different, just with enough money to act on the fantasies most of us have."

"Uh-huh." Ray sounded supremely unconvinced. "So, your dad and his brothers brought their wives here?"

"My dad's got four brothers," he said. "Only two of them—my uncles Dale and Darius—are married, leaving the other two to…sow royal oats."

Ray's laugher was short, but highly amused. "The

rich may be different, but they sure aren't boring." She turned to him then. "Did you want me to see this for a reason?"

"Well, you're here to check the place out, right? You don't want to have to tell E you missed a spot, do you?"

Ray took a short staircase up to a chaise lounge that was almost as wide as a twin bed. It was covered with a mass of silks and small round throws.

"You're right, I guess." Her response was wrapped in a teasing sigh. "I should be as thorough as possible." That said, she walked the length of the chaise. When she turned, she'd undone the robe's belt and waited.

Barker was already shaving off the distance between them. She didn't make the pursuit an easy one. When he came at her from one direction, she smoothly shifted to the other. Barker tired quickly of the play and simply reached across the lounge to snag a corner of the robe.

Ray merely shrugged off the garment and enjoyed the second or two she had to gloat before Barker cuffed her wrist in his palm. Any lingering traces of play failed. In an effortless move, Barker straddled the lounge and positioned Ray to straddle him. Her lashes flitted like hummingbird wings when her bare sex nudged his, still concealed beneath the gauzy powder-gray fabric of his sleep pants. In an instant, she was rocking in an attempt to absorb her fair share of sensation.

Barker took Ray's hips and mastered the determined sway of her body. The sensual rise and fall of her breasts before his face was a treat too tempting to resist. Her cry was a mix between gasp and shriek when he captured only the pouting tip of one breast into his mouth.

Ray bit her lip and, with both hands braced on the

back of the chaise, took in the sight of them in the mirrored ceiling. Barker's dark head moved eagerly against
her chest; his feasting there threatened to send her into
orgasm. Hands supporting her back, he kept her secure
as he sucked her nipples until they glistened and hard-
ened on his tongue.

Ray heard him moan then, and her heart made a
steady climb to her throat. When Barker flipped the
tables and put her beneath him, she didn't dream of
complaining—not when the view from that locale was
so satisfying. She was in a state of complete captiva-
tion as she studied the erotic flex of his heavily muscled
back. She was barely visible beneath his frame until he
began his descent to the part of her that ached for him.
Her hips left the tangle of vibrantly colored silks when
he used his index fingers to gently part the petal-soft
folds guarding her sex. His tongue filled her with a deep
and steady thrust moments later.

Greedily, she gripped and clutched the wondrous
source of stimulation. Her hands weakened by pleasure and just managed to cradle the back of Barker's
head as he delighted in her body. Between the vigorous tonguing and gentle nibbles to the moist folds at her
core, Ray tumbled fast and happily into the orgasmic
oblivion she anticipated.

Orgasm was not to be hers just then, though, and
she swatted at nothing but air when Barker withdrew
to leave her neglected on a cliff of stormy need. She
opened her eyes in time to see him reach into a deep
pocket of his pajamas and retrieve several condoms.
He tossed them to her stomach, the amusement in her
laughter taking a back seat to anticipation. Her mouth

went desert-dry when he freed the pants to send them gliding to the floor. He didn't return to the lounge, but stood behind its curved back.

Ray was sure to take one of the condoms when Barker tugged her down to meet him. She had it unpackaged by the time he had her calves over the back of the chaise. He set their protection in place, and Ray felt her heart in her ears then. She swore they'd popped when he clutched the bend of her knees and claimed her with a branding stroke. The thrust stretched, excited and satisfied to what Ray hoped would be no end.

The earlier voracity he'd used when taking her orally had adopted a leisured but no less arousing pace. Ray gripped the edges of the lounge and forbid herself to come no matter how fiercely her body raged for her to do exactly that. She didn't believe she'd ever see a more stunning sight than their mirrored images in the throes of vigorous sex. Still, her eyelids felt weighted, drugged, yet she remained lucid.

Her hips elevated and were in a superb position to experience each surge of every climactic wave. To be claimed in such a manner…there was no comparison for such stimuli. She pleaded when he spread her wide to increase penetration and pleasure at once. She couldn't hold off the inevitable for much longer. Barker seemed to sense that.

"Don't try it," he warned.

Again, Ray's breathless and anticipation-laced laughter filled the room.

There was a great deal to do over the next several days of their stay. The skies didn't clear much, but they did brighten enough during the day. Barker decided they probably wouldn't have a better time to be out and about.

Ray was all for it. Her exhaustion and queasiness even eased off some so that she could enjoy the sights and activity of the famous skiing oasis. There was a lot to be said for traveling with one's very own tour guide.

"The family tried to organize trips here at least once every other year when I was a kid," he told her once their server had left them with tall mugs of cocoa. "We usually came during the spring though. Winter trips were more complicated to arrange. Then there was the whole leaving snow for *more* snow for some of us."

"What?" Ray queried, smiling at the easy grin coming to his face.

"It's funny because the winter trips are the ones I remember most."

"I can see why." Ray breathed in the crisp mountain air. "I bet it was a treat seeing all this decked out—with the gondolas all around, trees all lit and shining from the mountains." She squeezed the large mug in her mittened hands. The smell of real Swiss cocoa seduced her nostrils, and she surrendered to the sliver of decadence in her bones.

Rayelle and Barker enjoyed their hot beverages from a table at a small café. There, they took in the sky's subtle transition from overcast day to night. Due to the cloudy conditions, the festive lighting had remained active for much of the day. Ray considered it a treat to watch the lights turn more vivid with the onset of evening. Barker had settled back to enjoy the view, as well. His posture was a relaxed one against the cushioned chairs. To provide even more pampering, leather settees accompanied the chairs for an added layer of comfort should one decide to prop up their feet while taking in the view. Barker took full advantage of the amenity, necessary after another day of sightseeing. That day had even been capped off by shopping.

"Coming here during the winter was my favorite because it was the only time everybody seemed to get along," he shared. "It was like something magical came down and wiped everybody's mind free of whatever it was that kept them at each other's throats for the rest of the year."

Ray laughed, sipped her cocoa and enjoyed the way it fought the icy wind and microscopic snowflakes that hit her face. "I hear presents have a way of encouraging forgetfulness," she teased.

Barker grinned and sipped his cocoa. "True, but it was a little more than that." He shifted to an even more comfortable position in the chair. "I swear you could almost feel the love in the house. There was no mistaking it."

"You're a romantic, Barker Grant. Did you know that?"

"Maybe… I think I'm just hopeful when it comes to family. The potential is there, and I think we'll reach it, especially with new family making its way into the fold." He gave her a look before raising his mug in a toast.

Ray accepted and clicked her mug to his. "Thanks, Barker. I needed this."

"I know." Content, he returned to sipping his drink.

Ray shook her head, and the rest of the outing passed in happy silence.

* * *

Barker resisted the urge to open his eyes in the morning. They'd be leaving that afternoon.

Naturally, he wasn't ready for the trip to come to an end, even though he and Ray had seen and done just about all there was to do in the snowy village. Still, he wanted to embrace the serenity they'd found there, far away from the concerns and obstacles in their real lives. If he kept his eyes closed just a little longer...

There was movement close to him in the wide bed. He and Ray had taken to the loft room—another thing he'd miss when they left. With a sigh, he opened his eyes to find her there before him, looking as though she'd been waiting on him to awaken.

Smiling then, Barker's agitations over leaving fled. He reached out to tug a lock that had fallen from the messy ball she'd pulled her hair into. He wanted to wake up to her every day—it didn't matter where they were. The serenity he felt wasn't in a place; it was in the woman, *this* woman, whose toughness was tempered by an inner uncertainty that melted his heart.

"I'm in love with you, Rayelle Keats," he told her.

Ray squeezed her eyes shut, but there was no hiding the sheen of tears glistening in her expressive gaze.

"I'm in love with you, too," she said, "and you, um... you're going to be a father." She waved the pregnancy test module she'd picked up during their shopping trip the day before.

"I know," he said, barely glancing at the strip.

Ray smirked. "Now you have proof."

"And while I'm happy beyond belief, I know it upsets you."

"It's not that."

"What then?"

"It's hard to explain." She swallowed noticeably. "And harder to understand. I…"

"You're afraid."

"Not the way you think. I…my mother…she hated being a mother. I think she only kept me because she believed one day the man she thought would leave his wife for her would come back. I was her ace in the hole." She waved then, as if trying to dismiss an annoyance. "Sorry for going on about my mommy problems."

"Don't do that," he said, hating the torture filling her eyes. "Don't make light of what you feel."

Ray gave a watery laugh. "What your uncle said about provocative ways—it was something my mother used to say. A woman's *provocative ways* was all she ever needed. She told me a lady she used to work for lived by that code. I, um… I never asked what she did for the lady."

"Babe—"

"She was a lot like Miss J, you know? My mom…"

"She was?" Barker realized she needed to have her say.

Ray nodded. "She could have anyone. Hmph, she did have anyone. There was just one she wanted too much—a whole lot more than he wanted her…or me. For a long time I got by on the idea that at least she loved him. Why else would she keep me?"

Barker brushed his knuckles down her cheek.

"Her ace in the hole…but still a reminder that she wasn't so free anymore. I was baggage, and she made sure I knew it. I've been on my own since I was sixteen." She winced and looked his way then. "It's okay if you say it."

"Say what?" His focus was on the spot his thumb brushed along her collarbone.

"That it's past time for me to get over my hurt feelings."

Barker cupped her jaw. "You've got every right to your feelings, Ray. Never tell yourself otherwise." He gave her cheek a slight squeeze then. "Have you ever thought that maybe your mother was afraid of being alone with you to care for, and it messed with her ability to love you the way she should have?"

"Yeah...yes, it's occurred to me. A lot—a lot more since...this." She tapped the test strip to her palm. "What if what's in her is in me? What if I'm capable of treating my own child like garbage because I was alone or had a bad day? Being so awful that my child would pick the world over me? No." She shook her head fiercely.

Barker sat up, taking Ray's face between his hands. "Are you listening?" He waited for her to nod. "No matter what happens between us—that's not a decision our child will ever have to make." He squeezed her face again.

"You didn't pick just anyone to have a baby with, Rayelle." He smiled when she laughed, as he'd intended.

"I told you before that I care for what's mine—for what I love. When you decide to believe that, you'll know where to find me." With those words, he put his forehead to hers, and they remained that way for a while.

# Chapter 14

*Philadelphia, PA*
*Two days later...*

"What?" Ray asked on a laugh. She and Barker were back home and making good on the dinner date he'd requested.

Barker lifted a hand inches off the dining table and let it settle as coolly as it had risen. "I was sure I'd need to remind you of our date."

She wasn't surprised by his response and shrugged. "Not that I want to, but there's no sense trying to avoid our dates—especially the dinner-related ones." She ran a finger along the rim of her water glass. "I'm prepared for you to be my shadow until the baby comes."

*Longer than that.* Barker decided to keep the thought silent for the time being.

Ray looked longingly toward the glass of merlot Barker had ordered. She closed her mind to disappointment, knowing the feeling of sacrifice would only get worse over the next several months.

"So, tell me why we're here? Or why *you're* here, since I'm just a pretty face to help you maintain your cover." Teasing was bright in her voice then.

Barker smiled while scanning the LaMours dining room. "I think we've caught a break on the story," he said.

"Can you elaborate?"

Barker considered his wine while gathering his thoughts. "We have reason to believe that old buildings suddenly bought near the tracks are being used for illegal gambling dives. There's a chance that more than gambling is going on."

"Like what?" Small lines furrowed Ray's brow when she saw Barker was reluctant to share.

"With Jazzy B's changing its…focus, it leaves a wider market open."

"But there are tons of clubs—"

"Not like Jazzy B's and its clientele," Barker interjected before Ray could give her ready argument. "Suddenly without that preferred environment, someone's gonna want that business."

"That business sowed the seeds for a lot of trouble."

Barker nodded. "Seeds our DA and Chief of Detectives would weed out as soon as they see." He spoke of District Attorney Paula Starker and Chief of Detectives Sophia Hail-Rodriguez.

"And you think someone here knows about it?" Ray scanned the dining room then, as well.

"LaMours's head chef," Barker shared, his expression grim. "Steven Saltzman's gambling problems and love for the finer things ruined his marriage. It makes sense to me now why he was at my uncle's party."

"There's nothing wrong with wanting the finer things, Barker."

"I know that, and it's why I'm curious that Saltz would rather spend time at an illegal club in an area of town where the buses don't run instead of the restaurant he practically owns."

"Well, that's—" Ray stopped herself, catching sight of the approaching bodies in her periphery. The twenty-something couple apologized to Ray for the interruption and made quick work of telling Barker they were journalism students who hoped to model their careers after his. They rounded out their speech by asking Barker for autographs that he graciously provided.

"LaMour is what it is because of him," Barker went on, never breaking stride despite the adoration he'd just been showered with. "I don't get why he'd rather spend his time at a building on the verge of being condemned than here."

"Maybe he's branching out?" Ray tried. "Could be he's got plans for a restaurant of his own."

"I hope so." Barker raised his glass but studied the light shining through the deep red contents instead of drinking. "Otherwise he'd make for a fine source."

Ray was prepping for another question when she heard Barker's name. A tall, stout man approached, his round face brightened by a wide grin. Barker stood to accept his extended hand to shake.

"Not every day I get one of *the* Philly Grants in my place! How are you, man?"

Barker chuckled. "Can't complain."

"And I see why." The man's eyes turned to Rayelle. "Not with this beauty to enjoy a fine meal with. I see you took my advice about getting him here."

"Ray, you remember Steven Saltzman?"

Ray was already nodding and taking Saltzman's hand. "I remember, and yes, there was no way I was gonna let him forget to bring me here. Nice seeing you again," she said.

"It was good seeing you at my uncle's party, too," Barker chimed in.

Saltzman nodded. "Dean was nice enough to invite me." He referred to Dean Grant, Barker's cousin. "We met right here at LaMours."

"Nice to know the fool actually left work to eat."

Saltzman grinned. "That's exactly what he said about you being at his dad's party."

There was laughter all around, but then Ray felt her heart lurch unexpectedly when Barker looked to her and winked. Fortunately, she soon grasped that it was a message that his plan was about to take off, instead of a sexy gesture meant to unbalance her.

"Guess I haven't been as 'on the job' as I should be," Barker admitted.

"I hear the Bahamas'll do that to you," Saltzman mused.

Barker rolled his eyes. "I won't be part of the other half for long if I keep tapping out the way I did at the tables down there."

Awareness crept into Ray's eyes as she watched Saltzman take the bait.

"The tables, huh?" he jibed.

Barker shrugged. "I only need a taste every now and then." He brushed the back of his hand down Ray's arm. "Glad I had this one with me to pull me back."

"Did I really?" Playing along then, Ray hiked a brow. "You lost over twenty-five k down there, remember?"

Barker feigned a bashful look. "And that's when she was with me," he told Saltzman.

"Anyway." Ray sighed and reached for her purse. "I'm headed for the powder room. 'Scuse me, gentlemen."

"She's right," Barker said once Ray had left them. "I've gotta do better. That trip almost wiped me out, and it's a long time 'til payday rolls back around."

"Like I said, how the other half lives." Saltzman grinned as a speculative look sharpened his features. "Maybe what you need is a spot closer to home."

Barker shook his head. "What I need is to quit while I'm ahead. This is a road I don't want to go down. No one should when they've pulled themselves out of crap to land in a pretty good spot."

Saltzman appeared to be reading Barker's expression when the reporter scanned the dining room, which was decked out festively. "You came here to pump me for information, didn't you?"

"What is it you think I expect you to know?"

"Don't treat me like an idiot, Barker."

"What's goin' on out there where the buses don't run, Saltz?"

"Walk away from this." Steven Saltzman's expression was as level as his words.

Barker responded in kind. "I can't do that," he said.

"Neither can you. You practically run this place, Saltz. Your name's synonymous with it."

"For being a servant," Saltzman grumbled.

"Artist," Barker countered.

Saltzman winced, moving closer to Barker. "I'm rubbing elbows with people you wouldn't believe now."

"Isn't that what you do here at LaMours?"

"*There,* I'm an equal."

"And when you lose?" Barker tilted his head when the other man looked away. "You know that's coming, too, right?"

"Losing is part of it. I can handle myself. I've learned…" He gave a fast, stubborn shake of his head. "It won't be like it was before."

"Stay away from it, Saltz."

"Go to hell, Grant," Saltzman hissed, keeping his voice at the fierce level when he next spoke. "Do you really think you'll stop it? There will be a new club the day after you think you've won."

"Then I'd deal with it then."

"Life of the rich," Saltzman continued to muse. "You people think you can *fix* anything that doesn't fit in with your perception of morals." He pursed his lips and looked disgusted. "So busy looking at everyone else, you don't see what's right next to you. You should let this go, Bar."

"And you should know I won't. I'd really like for you not to be around to see what's coming, Saltz."

"What are you?" The edge to the other man's query was underscored by a quick shot of laughter. "The Ghost of Christmas Present? Here to spread goodwill and save me from myself?"

Barker saw Ray wave to him, and he pulled money from his pocket to handle the check. He squeezed Saltzman's arm. "Somethin' like that." He smiled and looked back at the table. "Excellent meal as usual. Merry Christmas, Saltz."

"So, he basically confirmed it?" Ray watched Barker in disbelief from the Jeep's passenger seat. She studied Barker across the gearshift.

"More or less." He sighed, his head resting along the seat back, his mouth a thin line as he spoke.

New realization brightened Ray's eyes. "But that's not really why you wanted to see him, is it?"

Barker's shoulder rose in a half shrug. "I don't really want to see the guy ruin his life again. It was bad for him before."

"So, you didn't want him for a story?"

Barker smirked. "He would've been a great source, but sometimes there're more important things. He doesn't need the trouble sure to come his way when the place is taken down."

Ray punched his shoulder and smiled when he looked her way. "You're some kind of reporter," she said.

"Soft?"

"Compassionate."

"Like I said, you didn't pick just any guy to have a baby with."

Ray shook her head and settled back into her seat. For a while, she enjoyed the streets, which presented a spectacular display of lights hailing the season. Suddenly, she bolted up in her seat. A hand covered her mouth as her light eyes widened.

"Ray?"

"Take this exit," she said.

"Sorry it's so late, guys," Ray apologized as the four girls dragged themselves into the cozily decorated living room of Endeavor House.

"I really only had a few questions for Suze." She nodded to Suzanne Jessup. "Thought it'd help to have you guys with her..." Ray trailed off as she realized her explanation was going unheard.

The girls were far more intrigued by the man who had accompanied their mentor to the meeting. Ray made quick introductions and allowed her young friends time for drooling and silent adoration.

Ajani Pinkney was first to approach Barker with an outstretched hand. "We know who you are. We watch the news on WPXI every night. Um...almost every night."

"I'm impressed." Soft laughter etched Barker's words. "I'm not even on camera," he said.

Bettina Franks was next to move in, casually nudging Ajani aside as she did. "She means we watch *After-News* on WPXI."

Across the room, Ray watched the scene play out. Her head inclined thoughtfully as she smiled. *After-News* was a behind-the-scenes show on WPXI's cable affiliate. The show offered an inside look at how the network's most probing stories were produced. Barker and his team were regular fixtures, as the station's most suspenseful stories seemed to come from their camp. For someone who went out of his way to keep his striking face off-screen, Ray thought, the screen found a way. If the young women currently gazing dreamily at Barker Grant were any example, the WPXI viewing audience couldn't be any happier.

Ray let the girls adore Barker for another minute, before she cleared her throat to weigh in over all the chatter and breathless giggles. "Guys, we didn't come to stay long," she called out. "It's late, and you all need to be getting back to bed."

The girls disagreed, of course, and flashed quick looks of annoyance in Ray's direction.

"Barker?" Ray's tone was pleading.

He nodded. "Ray's right, girls. I'm sorry," he said in a soothing tone, as a melee of whines hit the air. "When the lady's in a rush, what's a guy to do?" He teased at Ray's expense and was successful at coaxing laughter from his young audience.

"Thanks," Ray remarked flatly, though a smile held her lips, as well.

Barker's manner took a serious turn. "Listen, girls, we really do need your help."

Frowns began to take shape subtly across the pretty faces of the young women. Concern merged when they looked to their mentor.

"Are you all right, Ray?" Leona Best asked.

"Oh, I'm fine, sweetie." Ray gave the girls a reassuring wave from where she stood. Then she looked to Suzette. "Suze, honey, I need you to tell me about the club."

Panic swam in Suzette Jessup's eyes, and was followed swiftly by a look of betrayal. "You promised," she whispered, moving from the huddle she and her friends had made around Barker.

"Honey, please understand, I—"

"No, Ray. You promised."

Ray braced herself to try again, but knew the attempt was useless. She all too easily remembered herself at that age. The reasons were irrelevant—all that mattered was the broken promise.

"Suzette?"

Ray blinked, hearing Barker's soft baritone filling the room.

"I don't know you very well," he was saying, "but I know Ray, and she never meant to betray you. She didn't want to come to you with this, but she's concerned."

Suzette hung her head and sighed. "I told her I was okay."

"You may be for now. Thing is, we think your job is a place the cops could be coming down hard on in a few weeks."

"Why?"

Barker shook his head. "Could be an off-the-books gambling dive for one—"

"Barker—" Ray called to him in a cautionary tone.

"She should know this, Ray," Barker countered with another shake of his head. "Last thing she needs is to be booked along with the rest if it comes to that."

"Booked?" Ajani squealed, balling her fists. "I knew that place was shady."

"Tell them what they want to know, Suze!" Leona cried.

"There's nothing to tell!" Suzette threw back. "All I do is serve drinks—I swear." She made the plea to Barker. "They don't make a big deal about age there so…" Awareness took shape in her eyes then. "Is that what this is about?"

"With everything that's gone on here in town lately, the tolerance level is nonexistent for anything that smells funny," Barker warned. "The cops aren't playing any games, and gambling could be just the beginning if all my team is uncovering is true. Sooner or later your employer will cross too many lines, Suzette. It'll be the end of them and anyone unlucky enough to be associated with them." He sent a soft look toward Rayelle.

"Ray cares about you. She's told me enough about all of you, and now you've got me caring, too. As for Ray, I don't like to see her upset—and this is going to do that until it doesn't, so…"

Suzette nodded slowly, as if to accept that the ball was in her court. "What do you want to know?"

"The address," Ray said.

"And if it's the one you're looking for?"

"That's up to you," Barker answered, even though Suzette had posed the question to Ray. "Rayelle believes in you—all of you. She thinks you guys will go a lot further than where you are now."

"What about the other girls working there?" Suzette asked, concern abounding in her tone and expression. "They aren't crooks, and some of them need the job more than I do. What happens to their kids without the job?"

"What happens to the kids if their parents are in jail?" Bettina threw back.

Suzette worried her thumbnail between her teeth. "That could happen anyway if the place is still in business."

"This isn't about ruining people's fun or, more importantly, their lives," Barker said. "If it's just gambling, they could run it as a private party in the city, but to go this far…it's a safe enough bet that there could be more involved."

"Jeez, Suze, would you just tell them already?" Leona blurted.

Suzette looked to Ray again. That time, her eyes brimmed with apology, which she cried out while running to tightly embrace her mentor.

"Shh…it's all right," Ray soothed, brushing a kiss to Suzette's temple.

Suzette pulled back. "Giving you the address won't work," she said.

Ray nodded. "It's okay, sweetie." She tugged at the edge of the scarf around the girl's wrapped hair. She made herself accept that they hadn't convinced Suzette of how serious the situation was. If the matter were over anything other than what it was, Ray could've admired her spunk.

Suzette was smiling. "Don't worry, Ray. I'll give you the address." She squeezed Ray's hand and then looked to Barker. "But I want to do more than that," she added.

"You okay with this?" Barker asked.

Ray smiled with a playful weariness. "Be careful what you wish for, right? We only wanted her to confirm an address. Not crack open a possible scandal."

"We'll have eyes on her the entire time." Barker squeezed Ray close as they strolled the walkway outside the Endeavor House entrance. "You should be proud. They're a fine group of girls."

"Yeah." Ray's smile was genuinely content. "They'll do things the right way."

"Unlike who? You?"

"I could've done things a lot better—a lot differently. I had too many stars in my eyes, thinking the world had something better to offer than what I already knew— that there was a prince to carry me away from all this. I should've been smarter."

"Okay. Although, if you had, you may never have wound up here, making sure four girls ended up some-place better."

Ray gave him a quirky look when she angled her head back up at him. "Are those your reporter's senses kicking in again?"

"Doesn't take anything but to observe."

"I started volunteering here right after Miss J put me in management at Jazzy B's." Ray turned her face up toward a frigid breeze that swept in. "It was like some kind of therapy at first—therapy for me, I mean." She shoved her hands deeper into her coat pockets and walked on ahead of Barker.

"I needed to prove to myself that I wasn't the only teen who'd ever found herself at a crossroads. It can be easy to believe that when you're preoccupied by your own drama." She perched on the back of a wooden bench near the end of the walkway.

"They helped me as much as I helped them—saw something in me I didn't see in myself and…" She shrugged. "I think that's when my real therapy began. Somewhere along the way I got sidetracked—*preoccupied,* more like, with showing the girls what their futures *could* be instead of focusing on what their realities were. Maybe if I'd focused on the reality, I would've known Suze wanted to work and gotten her a better job that—"

"Whoa." Barker was there at Ray's side, taking her arm. "That's not your weight to carry."

"I don't know about that—what if showing them the finer things of life made Suze rush to have it, and in a way she shouldn't have? It doesn't work to dwell on fantasy."

"Sometimes fantasy leads to hope," Barker mused.

"And what about reality? Hope doesn't make it disappear."

"But it can make the reality better, can't it?"

Before she could answer, Ray felt something cold land against her cheek. Snowfall. Another gust of the frigid breeze blew several more flakes into her face, and she laughed.

"I guess that's a yes to your question!"

"And what about this question?"

Ray was still laughing when she looked down and saw the streetlight bouncing off a box. She squinted, realizing it wasn't the box that was illuminated, but the crescent-shaped stone inside it.

"Barker…"

"I'd really like to hear you say you'll marry me."

"Barker, I—just because I…you don't have to do this."

"I actually do. I've been carrying this around in my pocket since Switzerland."

Ray only gaped.

Barker tilted his head, looking more directly into her face. "Since before I left here for Switzerland."

She understood. He wanted her to know his plans

had been made before the news hit that they were to be parents.

"Do you love me, Rayelle?"

Hand covering her mouth as emotion surged to an overwhelming crest, she nodded. "I do." She shuddered. "I have since *before* I took that test in Switzerland."

Barker chuckled, understanding the clarification. "I don't mind giving you time to think on it." He shifted his weight from one foot to the other as he studied the ground.

"Since you're going to say yes anyway—" he joined in when he saw her smile. "I'm happy to take my answer now."

"Well—" she pretended to be slightly confused "—considering what you just said about hope—I'd think you'd want a little more time to enjoy that part."

Barker drew her close. "Hoping has its fun parts, but sometimes you just need to go straight to the reality." He kissed her in a quick, heated manner before pulling back.

"Would it help if you wore the ring?"

She gave him a sad smile. "I'm afraid it won't."

Barker nodded. Small furrows tugged the sleek lines of his brows, and he appeared to be trying to reign in impatience. Ray moved closer, propped a finger beneath his chin and waited for his dark eyes to settle on her lighter ones.

"Wearing your gorgeous ring won't help me make up my mind, because I've already made it." She nodded then, laughter forming as she watched his expression brighten.

"Yes, Barker Daniel Grant. Yes, I'll marry you."

He tugged her close, eyes looking weighty with apparent relief as he put his forehead to hers. "How is it you know my middle name?" he asked.

"Your mom might've mentioned it when we had a few minutes together at the party while you weren't hovering."

Laughter drifted between the engaged couple. Soon, however, Barker was interrupting for more kissing. The wind and snow had picked up around them, and Ray gasped in the midst of it all when she felt the cold platinum ring band slide onto her finger.

She gasped a third time when she took notice of a wide window along the second floor of Endeavor House. She broke Barker's kiss and pressed her forehead to his again.

"We've got an audience," she whispered, referring to her young mentees. The girls were crowded in the living room window and beaming down at the couple embracing in the moonlight.

Barker didn't turn to observe the audience. Instead, he leaned down to swing Ray up into his arms. "The least we can do is give our guests a good show."

"Not too good," Ray cautioned. "This is a PG-13 crowd," she added.

Barker winced and then favored his fiancée with a wink. "It's Christmas. Let 'em live a little." He gave her mouth a loud smack beneath his, and then proceeded to gnaw at her neck.

Ray giggled hysterically while Barker whisked them into his car and out of the snowy, special night.

# Chapter 15

*Four days later...*

Monika Adair Grant was among a select few people in the world who had never felt the least bit slighted by having her birthday fall near the biggest holiday of the year. She'd actually considered it something of an honor, and one worthy of being abundantly celebrated, even if those closest to her did tend to use it as an excuse to be a touch stingy with her birthday gifts.

Luckily, Monika always believed it was the celebration that counted. Her family and friends had always done a phenomenal job with that.

The Grant family's annual Christmas party was a prime example. Soon after Monika had married the love of her life, Davius Grant, his mother, Gwyneth Grant, had suggested—decided, really—there wasn't a more appropriate place to hold the large end-of-the-year bash than at the home of her eldest son and his wife. As much as Monika had adored her mother-in-law, she'd always figured the woman had locked on to a clever way to avoid having her own home turned upside down for the festivities. Monika didn't mind; after all, a party was a party. And when it encompassed her birthday, it was an event beyond spectacular.

Such could be said of the night's gaiety. Monika Grant's home was vibrant, with the sounds and sights of the season. The guests, numbering well over seventy-five, socialized throughout the vast lower level, hugging, laughing and chattering away. The fragrance of apple cider, spices and chestnuts mingled in the comfortable warmth. A five-member jazz ensemble filled the space with Christmas classics that had many gravitating toward the makeshift dance floor that had taken over the den.

Something of a challenge had been issued from the older guests to those who were at least ten years their junior. With the upbeat and infectious holiday rhythms of the ensemble leading the way, the challenge was accepted as a battle between the ages ensued. Good cheer abounded, mixed with abundant laughter.

Among those who had taken to the dance floor were newlyweds Rook and Viva Lourdess. The couple had arrived just that morning from their home in Cortina, Italy. The unexpected visit from the talented actress and her husband had thrilled their families, as well as Viva's local fans. Also burning up the dance floor were her sister and brother-in-law.

Newlyweds Santigo and Sophia Rodriguez were a lively duo as they tackled the floor with eye-catching precision. Their moves garnered more than a few approving whistles. Not to be outdone, newly engaged Elias Joss and Clarissa David pulled in their fair share of cheers and applause. They treated the onlookers to an energetic routine full of twists and flips that kept Clarissa off her feet.

Eli had decided against waiting for an outrageously fabulous proposal trip. Ray discovered he had popped the question to her best friend the day after she'd left for Switzerland.

The other two newly engaged couples on the festive premises that evening decided to forgo the dance challenge—for a while anyway. Barker carried on a boisterous chat with his old friend Linus Brooks. Meanwhile, Linus's fiancée, Paula Starker, enjoyed watching the entertaining couples on the dance floor with her new friend Rayelle.

"What's that for?" Ray laughed when Paula shook her head.

"If anyone—and I don't care how reputable they are—if *anyone* had told me two years ago—hell, *one* year ago—that we'd all be here this way…happy and with all drama and misunderstandings over and done with…" She shook her head again.

"I would've used all my power as the DA to have them committed."

Ray laughed a while longer. "I don't think I'd have believed it if someone told me all this six *months* ago."

Again, Paula nodded and then sighed. "Ray, girl, are we all crazy?"

"I'd say that's a no as far as you and Linus are concerned."

"Why just me and L?"

Ray shrugged. "You've got history. If it weren't for the misunderstandings, you'd have been married years ago." She shook her head then. "I don't know what me and Barker are doing. It's all like—like a blur."

"A happy blur?" Paula punctuated the query with a coy smile.

Ray couldn't help throwing back her head for more laughter. "A stupid, happy blur!"

"You're on the right track, Ray—trust that." Paula tapped Ray's arm when she noticed Barker heading toward the stage. "Looks like your fiancé's got something to say."

Ray whirled around. "He wouldn't." She groaned after a moment.

Linus, seated nearby, had apparently overheard Ray. "He would," Linus confirmed and pulled Paula to her feet in order to take his place in the chair she'd occupied. He settled Paula onto his lap.

Ray could only shake her head, watching as Barker tapped the mic to check that it was engaged. A second later, his rich, well-known voice was resonating across the soft golden-lit room.

"Sorry for the interruption, folks," he said. "We'll get back to the music soon, but there's just something I need to say. Rayelle? Would you come up here please?"

Linus and Paula turned broad grins in Ray's direction. Ray, meanwhile, took a beat to close her eyes and prepare.

"Shut up," she grumbled to Linus and Paula while moving to her fiancé.

"Sorry for breaking my promise," Barker was saying into the mic while the crowd parted for Ray. "My mom's just asking for way too many hints about her birthday present that she hopes won't be her Christmas present. I don't think it'll hurt much if we give her part one now, do you?"

Hearty laughter rumbled around the room when a delighted squeal came from the area where the birthday girl's table sat on a high platform off from the stage.

"By now," Barker continued, "everyone knows that Ray's best friend and one of my best friends just got engaged. I wish you guys all the best."

Applause and cheer rose for Eli and Clarissa. Barker resumed his speech as the volume dropped. "What you guys probably don't know is if it weren't for E and Clarissa, Rayelle and I might not have met, or had excuses to keep seeing each other so we could become friends... so we could become more."

Ray was at the stage by then, assisted up by a member of the jazz ensemble. Barker took her hand and drew her with him to the mic.

"A few days ago, I asked this vision to be more than my friend. I asked her to be my wife—"

Cheers, applause and more squealing filled the room before Barker could finish.

"And she said yes!" he called out over the exuberant crowd.

Ray could feel her cheeks burning, aching behind the smile she felt taking hold of her face. Surprisingly, she didn't want the moment to end. Instead, she wanted to relish it.

Applause continued to erupt in a wild outpour. Then Barker raised a hand to request silence. When it began to take hold of the room, he turned to Ray.

"The first night we shared the table in that overcrowded restaurant, I never thought I'd be standing here about to share my life with you." He pulled her close, speaking near her ear so that only she could hear. "About to share *this* life with you." He gave her waist a squeeze.

Ray understood the unspoken message and felt her eyes dampen. Barker followed the squeeze to her waist with a tender kiss to her mouth, and applause flooded the room once more.

Following the announcement, Ray spent much of her time being hugged and congratulated. She discovered that not all of Barker's family were the overprivileged snobs she'd at first assumed. In fact, among the vast number of Grants in attendance at the party, she met none who seemed to scoff at the idea of her and Barker's engagement.

From everyone, there were best wishes, as well as invites to dinner to get to know each other. Considering her fiancé's preference to maintain a comfy distance from his family, Ray figured it might take some doing to convince her workaholic sweetheart to accept some of the offers. Some of the invites, she discovered, were only meant for her. She realized this when a trio of Barker's uncles collected around her near one of several open bars at the party.

Leon Grant was the last to step back from the embrace his brothers had already enjoyed. "You just let us know a good time to stop by the club for those hot toddies, all right, Miss?"

Ray laughed. "I'll check to see when Barker's free."

"Don't trouble yourself with that, lovely." Anton Grant was already shaking his head. "The kid still has too much work on the brain to take time for fun."

"I don't know…" Darius Grant gave his brother a smirk. "He definitely took time out to woo this beauty. I'd say there's hope for the boy."

"I still say, give Rayelle a few years to work on mellowing the kid." Leon sent Ray a wink. "Then we work on including him in our outings."

"No way." Barker's voice filtered in as he approached the cozy group. "My wife goes nowhere without me—especially not with the three of you."

The uncles made a show of being offended with eye rolls and waves, but Ray could see it was all in fun. The threesome wished her luck in mellowing their nephew and then plied her with more kisses and welcomes to the family. They left their nephew with playful slaps to the back of his head, before taking their drinks and moving deeper into the party.

"They're hilarious!" Ray cuddled into Barker. "Your family's not so bad, actually."

"No, they're not." Barker's expression changed split seconds later. "But there are times when they do test my patience."

Ray looked up to take in his glare. Her expression changed then as well when she saw what fueled it.

Dean Grant approached with hands outstretched in a

gesture of what appeared to be surrender. "I only came to say congratulations—" he looked to Ray "—and that I'm sorry. What my father said was wrong. What *I* said was wrong."

Ray smiled. "Thank you, Dean."

"Where's your dad?" Barker asked his cousin.

Dean's mouth quirked on the verge of a smile. "I think Aunt Monika said she'd kick his ass if he showed up with any nonsense, so he decided to play it safe and told my mom to go on without him."

Laughter made a quick surge among the group. Soon, however, Dean was extending his hand.

"Truce?" he said.

Barker accepted the shake and threw in a grin. Dean went one better and drew his cousin into a quick hug. Next, he leaned down to put a kiss to Ray's cheek.

"Welcome to the family, Rayelle. Hope you know what you're getting into," he added with a chuckle.

Barker responded in kind. "Amen. Thanks, D."

Dean nodded. "Merry Christmas," he said before moving on through the party.

"Looks like your mom isn't a woman to be crossed," Ray said.

Barker laughed. "We've all learned it's best not to," he said while pulling Rayelle close.

The couple embraced, swaying in place to a jazz sax piece that floated on the air. The tune managed to carry the flavor of the holiday season and a sultry aura in the same chord. "I love yous" were exchanged. Shortly after, the distinct squeal was heard.

Monika Grant squeezed her son and his fiancée in a crushing hold. "I couldn't have asked for a better gift!"

Ray and Barker traded happy, meaningful looks, but made no mention of part two of their surprise.

"I already have the rooms picked where you'll stay tonight—"

"Ma—"

"Hush, Bari, you'll have plenty of time alone with her." Monika steamrolled her only child's arguments with scarcely a wave. "It's my birthday so that means— at least for tonight—I get what I want."

"You just got what you wanted—a daughter-in-law," Barker reminded her.

"Correct. And now I want to have her with me for breakfast. Now—" She turned to Ray with a flour- ish. The flowing chiffon and silks of her mauve gown swayed with graceful flourish. "Bari can sleep in his room, and you, Miss Ray, will have the suite next to mine. It's all ready  "

"Ma—"

"Let me know if there's anything you need—"

"Ma!"

"Oh! Hello there! Glad you could make it." Monika whisked off to greet additional guests and left her son shaking his head while Ray laughed.

"You told me it was best not to cross her," Ray said through her laughter.

"So—" she tugged him into a rocking embrace "—when do you plan to give her the second surprise?"

"We'll keep it quiet 'til things calm down after this thing." He kissed the tip of her nose.

"Sounds good." Ray tucked into his chest and smiled.

Barker sighed. "Yeah, we'll definitely need some- thing to get her to forgive us for ruining her party."

Ray's smile showed traces of strain when she noted Barker's changed tone. But she didn't have the chance to question it.

"Grant!"

Ray turned, as did several nearby guests. She saw three men she didn't recognize elbowing their way through the dense crowd. She could see one man looking well-past weary, while the others appeared livid.

"What the hell have you done?" Willard Harold demanded when he and his companions had closed in on Barker. "You've gone too far this time!"

Barker fixed WPXI's programming execs with a bland look. He then moved that look to the man bringing up the rear of the group. "Is that why you put all this in motion? My supposed threats to get me to back off the story? Came from you two, didn't they? Made the board extend that outrageous offer so they wouldn't lose me."

"That's insane." Harold's partner, Garrett Cole, seemed incapable of further speech.

"Is it?" Barker grimaced. "Is that why you brought your attorney to my mother's birthday party?" He observed Wesley Frakes.

Garrett Cole spoke again. "If it hadn't been for Wes walking in on your little thief, we never would've—"

"What the hell did you snakes do to her?" Ray moved in, her eyes blazing.

Cole ignored the query. "I expected more from you, Grant," he said instead, smirking after a lurid appraisal of Ray's face and form. "Having your flavor of the month getting one of her little tarts to spy for you is in such poor taste—"

Barker lunged, but found himself gripped by Rook. "No need for that, man. They'll be hurting well enough, and soon."

"You tell me what you did, you pig, or that hurt will come sooner than you think." Ray all but snarled the threat.

The seething intensity of her promise seemed to have the necessary effect. Cole seemed to cower as he retreated half a step. "We didn't do anything! The little—" He appeared to caution himself, as though realizing his intended words would result in true pain. "The young lady got away before Wes could retrieve our property. But we know she took something—"

"Right…you know exactly what she took," Barker accused then, inclining his head. "Thanks, Rook," he said and waited for Rook to ease his hold.

"That property is why I'm suddenly looking at a promotion, isn't it?"

Cole appeared to swell with fury. "I'm sure I don't know—"

"Your property is why you're asking me to let my team close out this story—close it out before we discovered you two own the very *property* we're investigating."

"Lies," Harold breathed.

"*That's* the lie," Barker countered. "I can produce what's been a suspiciously hard-to-find deed to that property with the names of you two bozos typed and signed all nice and neat across the bottom. Not to mention surveillance footage of the exterior and interior, and all the terrific and illegal things going on in there."

"You'll pay for this, Grant!"

Barker smiled in Garrett Cole's direction. "You and your partner should be more concerned with how *you'll* be paying." He nodded toward the security on hand for the party.

The men bristled at being escorted out, but it silenced their arguments.

With a sigh, Barker turned, an immediate grin brightening his fierce features at the sight of finding his friends at his back.

"Think we have a chance of doing anything that really matters here?" he asked once he locked gazes with Paula.

She shook her head and rolled her eyes away from the commotion as the men were led out of the room. "May take some doing." She huffed out a breath. "Considering the *way* you came by your evidence."

Ray shook her head. "I'm sorry, Paula."

"Small potatoes. We'll get 'em." Paula sighed.

Ray gave a quirky smile. "Some girls are just headstrong." She referred to her mentee, Suzanne Jessup, who had insisted on doing more regardless of hers and Barker's words cautioning her against it.

Paula grinned. "That's because we know that's what it takes to survive." She looked to Barker. "We'll pin it to them—not sure of the final outcome, but you can count on things being sticky."

"It's doubtful the WPXI board would keep them in their positions," Elias mused.

"Now that sounds like success to me." Santigo rubbed his hands together.

"Thanks for putting a gold star at the top of my case file," Paula cheered. "Stamping out trouble before it's had the chance to flourish." She gave a self-satisfied nod. "Not bad for a DA's last hurrah."

"Consider it a wedding gift," Barker said.

"But don't think that lets you off the hook for *our* wedding gift," Ray advised.

Hugs and laughter followed before the gang parted ways.

"I'm gonna have to beat the guests off with a stick for next year's party!" Monika raved later while she, Barker and Rayelle enjoyed eggnog by one of the three massive fireplaces on the lower level.

"Don't you have enough folks to beat down?" Barker, with his legs propped on a footstool, approved of the quiet. "I heard about your threat to Uncle Dale."

"Aw." Monika waved it off. "He called long before the party to apologize. I told him it didn't count until he said it face-to-face to you both."

"Oh, Mrs. Grant, that—it's water under the bridge now," Ray assured the woman. "I'd rather go into the new year with everyone having a clean slate."

Monika shook her head in wonder. "You couldn't have picked a better girl to marry."

"Ma, um." Barker shared a look with Ray. "Does that mean you think she'd make a great mom, too?"

"Well, of course! And I expect that to be next year's birthday gift—sooner if you like."

"Glad to hear you say that, considering…"

Silence settled after Barker's comment for only a short while. Soon, Monika was gasping, followed by what was fast becoming her trademark squeal. She scooted from her end of the love seat she shared with

Ray and joined Barker on the edge of his. She gripped his and Ray's hands firmly.

"Say it outright so I know I'm not imagining things," she ordered.

Ray did the honors. "I'm going to be a mom. Your son will be a dad. You'll be a grandmother or...whatever you want your grandchild to call you."

Monika was squealing anew and drawing both Ray and Barker into smothering embraces. When she set them away, her eyes were shining.

"Thank you." Her voice held a quiet reverence.

Barker moved closer. "It's all right, Ma."

"I know. I—I just wish your dad could be here."

Barker pulled his mother into a smothering embrace of his own. "He is, Mama. He is."

Monika shook her head again. "I need to go fix my makeup," she said in a pretend huff before rushing off.

"Looks like she's happy," Ray said.

Barker sighed. "*She* is, but I wonder how we can top ourselves for her gift next year."

The couple dissolved into a fit of laughter. Soon after, they were cuddling on the sofa.

# *Epilogue*

*Christmas, One Year Later*

There was a knock, and Ray heard her husband's voice floating into their bedroom.

"Are boys allowed?" Barker asked.

Ray finished brushing her hair. "Only if they're cute and think I'm the most beautiful woman ever."

Barker walked into the room lit by the colorful lights of the small tree adorning the space.

"We've got the cute part squared away," he said. "As far as I'm concerned, you're the most beautiful woman ever." He looked down at the bundle he carried. "That opinion may one day change for this guy."

"Well." Ray turned and relieved Barker of their son. "It's not today," she cooed.

Bakhai Grant gazed up at his mother. Ray felt her heart melt for the millionth time since she'd met the new man in her life. Barker pulled his wife near, and together they smiled down at their son.

"Is everyone here yet?" Ray asked.

"Debra's on the way with her folks."

Ray laughed. "I can't believe your uncle's coming to the dedication."

The couple was heading to a special dedication service for newborns at Monika Grant's church. Everyone had been invited, it seemed, including Ray's Endeavor House family. Her mentees were each completing their last years in high school. Two held coveted jobs at the new DA's office, courtesy of Paula. The others were on staff at the offices of Joss Construction. It had been a special year for Barker's and Rayelle's closest circle of friends, as well as co-workers. WPXI had hired new personnel to assume the newly vacated positions of Willard Harold and Garrett Cole, who were currently preparing for trial on charges ranging from illegal gambling to contributing to the delinquency of minors. As for the Jazzy B's franchise, Ray and Clarissa had decided the clubs would stand as nightclubs for the foreseeable future. Rayelle and Clarissa would take baby steps toward the dance studio. A Philadelphia location was currently being scouted, with construction to begin within two years if all worked out. The success of the school would determine whether others would follow. Nothing, however, overshadowed what Barker and Rayelle Grant considered to be the greatest success of their lives.

"Think we'll do right by him?" Ray's voice was quiet

as she smoothed her fingers over the wisps of onyx curls covering her son's head.

Barker nodded, pride radiating as he studied his little boy, who was lightly dozing. "We've been doing okay so far. I've got faith we'll keep that up."

Ray smiled at the new life surrounding her. She could feel happiness and love continuing its progressive swell inside her chest. She looked up at Barker, brushed a kiss to his jaw and said, "So do I. So do I."

\* \* \* \* \*

KIMANI
ROMANCE™

# COMING NEXT MONTH
## Available November 20, 2018

### #597 BACHELOR UNBOUND
*Bachelors in Demand* • by Brenda Jackson
International jeweler Zion Blackstone felt an instant connection to
Celine Michaels. When she shows up at his house in Rome claiming
kidnappers are after her, he offers the Hollywood producer's daughter his
protection…and passion. But a revelation could upend his chance with
Celine…

### #598 A LOS ANGELES RENDEZVOUS
*Millionaire Moguls* • by Pamela Yaye
Jada Allen's Christmas wish list is simple: her gorgeous boss. A-list talent
agent Max Moore counts on Jada to handle his life. Yet workaholic Max never
notices her until a makeover reveals the woman he's taken for granted. Will one
hot night shatter their working relationship or lead to something sweeter?

### #599 ANOTHER CHANCE WITH YOU
*The DuGrandpres of Charleston* • *by Jacquelin Thomas*
Retired Secret Service agent Landon Trent stuns
Jadin DuGrandpre with the announcement that
they're still married. Winning back Jadin's trust
won't be easy—especially when a trial pits the two
Charleston attorneys on opposite sides. But Landon
isn't giving up. Can they recapture what they once
shared?

### #600 HER MISTLETOE BACHELOR
*Once Upon a Tiara* • by Carolyn Hector
After a public breakup, CFO Donovan Ravens
plans to spend the holidays alone in a small-town
hotel. But science teacher British Carres has other
ideas for the space the sexy bachelor booked. As
they give in to their chemistry, a threat from the
past could keep them from finding true love…

# Get 4 FREE REWARDS!

## We'll send you 2 FREE Books plus 2 FREE Mystery Gifts.

**Harlequin® Desire** books feature heroes who have it all: wealth, status, incredible good looks... everything but the right woman.

FREE Value Over $20

# SPECIAL EXCERPT FROM

## ⒣HARLEQUIN®

*Jada Allen's Christmas wish list is simple: her gorgeous
boss. A-list talent agent Max Moore counts on Jada to
handle his life—and help him get through to his tween
daughter. Yet workaholic Max never really notices her
until a makeover reveals the vibrant woman he's taken
for granted. Will one hot night shatter their working
relationship or lead to something far sweeter?*

*Read on for a sneak peek at*
**A Los Angeles Rendezvous,**
*the next exciting installment in the
Millionaire Moguls continuity by Pamela Yaye!*

Her hands were shaking, but she grabbed her purse off the
mahogany table and forced a smile, one that concealed the anger
simmering inside her. "Max, you know what? You're right," she
said, nodding her head. "I'm a lowly administrative assistant. Who
am I to tell you what to do? Or advise you about how to parent your
daughter? I'm a nobody."

Max tried to interrupt her, to clarify what he'd said seconds
earlier, but Jada cut him off.

"*You* asked for my help, but the moment I disagreed with you you
decided my opinion was worthless, and now that I know how you
*really* feel about me, I can't work for you."

"You're twisting my words. I never said that."

"You didn't have to. I'm quite skilled at reading between the
lines…" Her voice wobbled, but she pushed past her emotions
and spoke in a self-assured tone. "I'll submit an official letter of
resignation first thing Monday, but consider this my two-week
notice."

Fear flashed in his eyes. "Jada, you can't quit. I need you. You're the heart and soul of Millennium Talent agency, and I'd be lost without you."

"Nonsense. You're the legendary Max Moore. One of the most revered talent agents in the city. You don't need me, or anyone else. You've got this, remember?"

Her mind made up, she turned and strode through the foyer.

Max slid in front of her, blocking her path. His cologne washed over her, and for a moment Jada forgot why she was mad at him. He licked his lips, and tingles flooded her body.

"You're quitting because I disagreed with you?" he asked, his eyebrows jammed together in a crooked line. "Because we argued about Taylor's outfit for her school dance?"

*No, I'm quitting because I love you, and I'm tired of pretending I don't.*

"Thanks for everything, Max. It was an honor to work for you. I've learned so much."

"I won't let you quit. We're a team, Jada, and I need you at the agency."

Scared her emotions would get the best of her, and she'd burst into tears if she spoke, Jada stepped past Max and yanked open the front door. He called out to her, but she didn't stop. Ignored his apologies. Increased her pace. Fleeing the million-dollar estate, with the feng shui fountain, the vibrant flower garden and the winding cobblestone driveway, she willed her heart not to fail, and her legs not to buckle.

Jada deactivated the alarm, slipped inside her car and started it. Anxious to leave, she put on her seat belt, then sped through the wrought-iron gates. In her rearview mirror, she spotted Max and his brothers standing on the driveway and wondered if they were discussing her dramatic exit. Jada dismissed the thought, told herself it didn't matter what the Moore brothers were doing. Max was her past, not her future, and she had to stop thinking about him. Gripping the steering wheel, Jada swallowed hard, blinking away the tears in her eyes.

*Don't miss* A Los Angeles Rendezvous
*by Pamela Yaye, available December 2018
wherever Harlequin® Kimani Romance™
books and ebooks are sold.*

# *Love Harlequin romance?*

## DISCOVER.

Be the first to find out about promotions, news and exclusive content!

Facebook.com/HarlequinBooks

Twitter.com/HarlequinBooks

Instagram.com/HarlequinBooks

Pinterest.com/HarlequinBooks

ReaderService.com

## EXPLORE.

Sign up for the Harlequin e-newsletter and download a free book from any series at **TryHarlequin.com.**

## CONNECT.

Join our Harlequin community to share your thoughts and connect with other romance readers!
**Facebook.com/groups/HarlequinConnection**

**HARLEQUIN®**

**ROMANCE WHEN
YOU NEED IT**

HSOCIAL2018

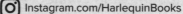